Meet the Teacher

MANDY MAREE

To all the teachers, I see you.
To those who have lost loved ones, I feel you.
To my husband and my two baby wildflowers, I love you

Content Warning

Dear reader,

Please note that though this book is labeled as a romantic comedy, there are some sensitive topics relating to the loss of a loved one to cancer and mental health conditions. The main character deals with a diagnosis of generalized anxiety disorder, and the experiences she has, mirror my own experiences and are not one-size-fits-all. There is also adult content relating to sex, and this book is best suitable for those who are age eighteen and over.

Lots of love to you all.

xo,
Mandy

1
The WOLO List

I stare at Zayn's lips—the ones he just used to shatter my heart into a million tiny pieces.

"I'm sorry, what?" I ask, hoping and praying I misunderstood him.

His eyes meet mine. We're so close that I can see the black pupils of his brown eyes despite the darkness surrounding us. A tear falls onto his cheek. "Trust me, this is the last thing I want to do. I want to be with you, Autumn, but . . ."

I freeze. "But, what? Why? I don't understand why you're doing this."

"Autumn, I—" A sigh escapes him. Zayn runs his fingers through his dark brown hair. "I'm truly sorry, but I'm not going to be at NYU with you. I, uh . . . I have to stay." He clears his throat. "I'm staying here."

"You're not going to school with me? Not moving with me?" My voice cracks. I search his eyes for answers. When he doesn't respond, I press for more. "So, what does that mean for us, then? Huh? Are you breaking up with me the day after our high school graduation? I,"—my voice shakes as I push the words out of my mouth— "I can't believe you're doing this to me."

Tears begin to flood my eyes, causing me to forget

we're standing in front of our school. We were supposed to be meeting to celebrate. My thoughts are in a race with one another. *Is he really ending us? He asked me to meet him at school so he could . . . break up with me? I thought he was the love of my life. Was that a goodbye kiss just now? One without warning? Why?*

He backs away, eyes filled with sorrow and regret.

I want to turn around and leave, but I can't help myself from wanting more answers. "Zayn, are you seriously doing this? Staying in this dump of a hometown we can't wait to leave? And with a man you hate?" My hands tremble as my arms make their way across my chest.

Zayn exhales. "Autumn, he's still my dad," he says.

"What the hell changed? I don't get it."

He shakes his head. "You won't get it, Autumn. I'm sorry we can't all have it so easy and just go run off into the sunset."

I scoff before the words fall out of my mouth. "It's not the sunset, Zayn. It's freaking college. You . . . got in. We had a plan. A plan, remember? We were going to live together after our first year in the dorms. How can you suddenly change your mind like this? And the day after our high school graduation?"

He runs his hands through his hair, releasing a sigh. "I wish I could explain it better to you, Autumn. I know I need to stay here. NYU isn't for a guy like me, anyway."

A knot twists its way into my stomach. I'm heartbroken and pissed.

"So, we're just . . . over?" I ask, allowing a heavy breath to leave my lips.

He nods. "Appears that way."

My whole body quivers, and my anxiety can't stop spiraling. I can't imagine life without him. What would my sister tell me to do right now? A salty tear makes its way to my lips. *Be strong, Autumn. No guy deserves your tears.* Realistically, I know she'd tell me what a douchebag he is, too.

Trying to summon my inner Summer, I lick my lips and wipe any remaining tears away.

"Fine." I say, yanking off the charm bracelet he bought for me on my eighteenth birthday. "Here, you can have this back, too."

He glances down at the bracelet I've thrown into his palm. "Autumn . . . it's not what I wa—ugh, forget it." He turns around and releases a sigh before he mumbles, "I still love you."

He pockets the charm bracelet before walking away. With each step he takes, it feels as though a part of my body is leaving with him. Maybe my heart.

He doesn't turn back around. After looking at my feet to verify I'm still standing, I lunge forward a bit and cover my hand with my mouth. I feel like I'm going to be sick. *Is this some kind of nightmare I can't wake up from?*

When the wave of nausea slightly subsides, I stow my hands in the pockets of my dress and lean up against the brick wall of the school. I slide down the wall until my bottom hits the ground. I want to curl up into a ball and die. The tears won't stop pouring out of me. I've never felt hurt like this before. My stomach feels like it's been hit with a soccer ball, leaving me in a struggle to catch my breath.

I start hoping that maybe this is all some sort of joke, or that maybe he'll realize what a stupid mistake he made and come right back. Vomit rises in my throat. Turning my head to the side to release it, I'm met with pain and relief simultaneously.

I unfold the flap of my crossbody purse, digging around

for a tissue or napkin. I pull out a crinkled-up napkin, instantly recognizing the logo of Eats & Sweets, a cute little coffee and donut shop we always hang out at. Well, used to. I sob into the napkin as someone's hand finds its way to my shoulder, startling me. *Maybe it's Zayn with a change of heart,* I think to myself for a second, heart full of hope. I grab a second napkin, using it to wipe my mouth and a few tears from my eyes. I look to my right. Rather than disappointment, comfort warms me at the sight of Mason's smile.

Mason and I have been best friends since the second grade. He's the one who convinced me to go through with my first date with Zayn, which I thought was a prank at the time. I never thought the captain of the football team would ever notice an average girl like me.

"Oh no, love. What's going on?" Mason asks. I see the concern written all over his face. More tears start to fall. I open my mouth to respond but only a gasp for air escapes it. It's still hard to breathe, let alone say a single word. Mason nods as he grabs another tissue out of my bag and hands it to me. I wipe the clumps of mascara and tears away.

"Hmph." Mason scoots closer. Noticing the pile of sick on the other side of me, he says, "Yikes, boo. You not feeling well or did something bad happen?"

"Something bad. Zayn dumped me. He's not coming with me to NYU." I want to tell him everything, but I can't find the words.

Mason's eyebrows furrow. "Damn boys, huh? Can't live with 'em, can't live without 'em." He pauses for a second before he adds, "I'm so sorry, Autumn. But I know you'll find your true love one day. I promise." He pushes my hair out of my face and begins to rub my back. Mason is a one-of-a-kind friend. We joke that he's a unicorn, and of course, he always specifies he's even better in that he's a *rainbow unicorn*. Rainbows and all, he always makes me feel so much more confident than I ever feel on my own . . . like I'm a unicorn, too. Although most of the time I feel more like a pony that people pay for people to ride at carnivals, fairs, and kids' birthday parties.

I rest my head on his shoulder for a while. When I finally manage to lift my head up a bit, I realize I've soaked his sleeve. I'm a mess. The only thoughts I have are of Zayn. *Why did he change his mind so suddenly? How could he do this? I thought we were perfect. We had a plan.*

I replay his words over and over again in my mind, letting it to slice my heart back open. I can't believe he's just . . .gone.

Mason hands me yet another tissue. I need to know the *why*. It'll kill me to never know. A terrible thought crosses my mind. "Hey Mason, can I ask you something?"

"Um, duh. What's up?" he asks.

"Do you think . . ." I muster up the courage to ask the question I didn't ask Zayn. "Ugh, do you think Zayn is staying because he . . . fell in love with someone else?"

Mason wraps an arm around me. "Oh, honey. I doubt it. That boy was completely smitten with you. He adored you and everyone around could see it. There's just no way he would've found someone else. And if he did, he's a douchebag who doesn't deserve you anyway."

"Hmph. I don't know. Maybe it was all just a lie."

"I understand where your head is at right now. But girl, I know you best. You're going to continually beat yourself up over this, forever asking yourself what you did wrong and why this happened to you. But sometimes we don't get that closure we need. You might never find out why he really decided to stay. What I can tell you is that if he really loves you, he'll come back. You know the saying 'let love go and that shit might come back' or whatever it is."

For the first time this evening, I laugh out loud. "I'm pretty sure that is not the saying."

He looks over at me and says, "But admit it, you know exactly what I meant."

I nod as my mouth forms a smirk. He's got a point.

"In the meantime," he continues, "let's work on you, girl. Forget about him. Need I remind you that you just graduated high school? You have a whole, unexplored road ahead of you that you haven't driven yet."

I know what Mason is saying is true. We just graduated high school no more than twenty-four hours ago. And he's right that I may never get any closure from this. My chest tightens as I swallow. *Stupid anxiety.*

"You're right. Ugh, but Zayn was supposed to leave after summer for college with me." More tears make their appearance as I choke out the words, "So, what if I never see him again?" My face gets hot as my mind races at the mere thought of never seeing him again.

"Autumn, I know this will sound harsh, but . . . well, who am I kidding? You know I'm always here for that tough love. Um, but—it's probably for the best. Just know that whatever is meant to be, will be. You're so strong, and I promise you'll survive without him. You've got me and Natalie!"

"I seriously don't know what I'd do without you two. But Mace, we won't be at the same school." The words come out as a whine as more tears threaten to spill out.

"Don't you dare start crying again. Everything is going to be fine, and you know it doesn't matter how far apart we all are, we're still your ride or dies." Mason releases me from his hold and adjusts his tie. "All right, girl, I'm done being Gandhi for the evening. Let's get you home now. Want me to walk with you?" He hops up and extends his hand for me.

Before I manage to grab it, Veronica Biltmore walks past us. She looks down at us and scoffs. "Took him long enough to realize what a nobody you are," she mumbles under her breath as she continues to walk on by.

Mason shoots me a look as if to say, *Oh hell, no!* But I shake my head, signaling to him it's no big deal.

"Ignore that bitch," Mason emphasizes the final word, and I'm hoping Veronica is still in earshot.

I wipe my tears one last time before reaching for his hand. I let out a huge sigh. "Thanks, Mason. Let's get outta here." I manage a smile, thankful for him being my knight in shining armor.

When we reach my house, I'm stunned to see my sister Summer on the porch swing, reading. Probably another romance novel—that's all she ever reads nowadays. I climb the steps to the porch. Summer looks up from her book, her eyes softening when they meet mine. She closes the book and jumps up from the swing, wrapping her arms tightly around me. I squeeze her back and my fingers entangle into her long blonde hair. The scent of her coconut shampoo fills my nostrils. Summer doesn't let go until I pull away.

"Tum Tum! What happened? You okay?" Her voice shakes, filled with concern. As my older sister, she's always been protective, even if she is the least serious of us. To emphasize me being the baby of the family, she nicknamed me Tum Tum; she's the only one who doesn't call me Autumn. And yes, my mom named us after the seasons—Summer and Autumn. She has always been asked if she had more children would they be named Winter and Spring, but she just laughs it off. I have a feeling she laughs because she's embarrassed that the answer is yes.

I shrug. Summer's eyes dart to Mason behind me. "Let's just say our baby girl will be going off to college single," he answers delicately.

Summer's jaw drops a bit as her eyes widen. "Are you serious? What an ass!"

Mason nods in agreement before rubbing my shoulder a final time and blowing us both goodbye kisses on the way back to his car. "Love you both!" he shouts before ducking inside it.

Summer gives me a squeeze and then walks me over to the porch swing where she was sitting. Having a big sister is tough at times, but I can always depend on her to be there for me. Summer is four and a half years older than I am. She finished up college in Denver and moved back home for the summer while she "figures things out." Summer and I are as different as day and night. She's always living from one adventure to the next, and I plan out everything as much as I possibly can. As prepared and excited as I am for college, I'm dreading what I'll actually do once I'm done with it. The mere thought of adulting plus all the added responsibilities of juggling a career, family, friends, and everything else overwhelms me. I quickly remind myself that it's not the time for my usual college-anxiety spiral. I'm sure it'll return another day.

We both take a seat on the swing, and she turns to me. "So, as much as I'm dying to know what actually happened, I'm first going to ask if you want to talk about it?"

I shake my head. "I know I eventually will, but honestly, for right now, do you think can we do something else instead? I think a distraction would be really nice to have tonight."

Summer's eyebrows raise as they always do when she's

processing or planning something. I can tell by the way her lips purse to her right cheek that she's formulating a plan for the night. I can sense it as well. We aren't twins, but I will say we share a lot of some sort of sister intuition, which comes in handy for when I'm indecisive. She somehow knows exactly what I want before I even know it myself.

Summer smiles. Not just any old smile though. The sparkle in her eyes indicates it's her idea smile. She stands up and extends her hand. Before I take it, I raise my brow in suspicion.

"Come with me. You know I always have the best ideas. Don't you trust that by now?" she asks with the cheesiest grin on her face.

"Fair enough," I say as I grab her hand, allowing her to pull me off the swing. We head inside, walking past our parents watching *Family Feud* on TV, and head straight to her bedroom. She slams the door behind us and her eyes shift around the room like she's on a mission to find something. She rummages through her desk drawer, pulls something out, and exclaims, "Aha! This is perfect."

A notebook? "Do you really think I want to journal right now? Cause let's be real, you and I both know I'll be doing that later anyway."

"No, silly. There you go again worrying for nothing," she says.

"OK. Fine. So, what's with the journal then?" I ask.

She grabs a pen from the coffee cup full of them on her desk. The one she chooses has a little yellow pom-pom on the top. "Get ready! We're going to make a YOLO list!"

"A what now?" I ask.

"Ugh." Summer rolls her eyes. "Do you even know who Drake is?"

"Well, of course I know who Drake is. But what is YOLO?"

Summer releases a sigh before she responds. "Sometimes I swear you live under a rock. I didn't think I'd have to explain it to you, but it's from Drake's newest song. YOLO—You Only Live Once. You really haven't heard the song yet?"

I grit my teeth and shrug. "Nope, sorry."

Summer waves me off with her hand. "Whatever, it's fine. Anyway, my plan is we make our own You-Only-Live-Once list." She pushes the pom-pom of the pen against her chin. "Wait, maybe it should be our WOLO list, short for We Only Live Once. That way we can create it together. What do ya think?"

Summer was right. This plan is distracting me. I haven't really thought much about Zayn since she's mentioned Drake and creating this weird YOLO—I mean, WOLO —list.

My lips form a slight smile. "Okay, fine. I'll admit I actually love it. Let's do it."

"Yes!" she exclaims. "I totally knew you would be down. But here's the thing. We have to do everything on the list before we're a bunch of old grannies with tons of regrets. Deal?" She pauses and adds, "I mean it, Autumn. You have to promise that you'll actually do this list with me."

Summer knows me so well. I'm hesitant to make that promise since we haven't even made the list yet.

"Okay, okay . . . but under one condition," I say.

She smirks. "Fine, what's the condition?"

"I'm willing to do whatever is on the list, but we have to both agree on it before you write it down. I want to feel like we're making a plan."

Her smile fades for a brief second before she nods in agreement.

Summer holds out her pinky for me. "Pinky promise?"

"Pinky promise."

"Alright then, it's settled. Let's get started."

Summer opens the notebook to a blank page. She writes at the top:

Summer + Autumn's WOLO List

2

☑ *Land Dream Job:*
Become a Teacher

*I*s it burned out or burnt out? I should know this. After all, I am a teacher. Ugh, I hate when people say shit like that, and here I am saying it. Well, whichever is correct—I've reached it.

I don't mean to brag, but I'm basically as burnt as toast when you put it at the highest setting. *Which by the way, does anyone actually use that setting? And if not, why do they even make such a high setting?*

"Ms. Parker, you appear to be frozen. Are you still there?" Principal Jane Montgomery, the lead interviewer, asks. *Shit.* I totally zoned out on this Zoom call. I really need to get used to being called Ms. Parker again.

"Yes, still here. I apologize, but I'm not sure what happened. I think my screen froze for a minute," I lie. *Not off to a good start here, Autumn.*

"That's alright. Would you be able to be here by August nineteenth for the start of our teacher workdays?" The principal asks as she awaits my response with a bright smile.

"Yes, I can definitely make that work," I answer.

She moves closer to the screen. "Wonderful, well we'd

love to formally offer you a position to join our fifth grade team! Welcome to Lake View Elementary! Or shall I say, 'welcome back'?"

"Thank you so much. I'm looking forward to a wonderful year there!" I lie again. Well, not entirely a lie. Now that I've lost my best friend—my one and only sister—I'm moving back to my hometown. It's the last place I want to be, but you've got to do what you've got to do sometimes, I guess.

Summer and I were opposites in so many ways, but we really were the best of friends. I think the icing on the cake of my gone-to-shit life is me and Liam getting divorced. So, perhaps I am hoping for a "wonderful year," but I'm realistically expecting to, at the very least, rise slightly above rock-bottom status. There's got to be a silver lining somewhere, right?

"It was a pleasure getting to know you a bit better today, Ms. Parker. We'll be in touch. See you soon." The woman inside the box on the screen waves at me, and the rest of the interview committee quickly mimics her.

"Thanks again. See you soon." I wave back, and it still feels awkward despite having taught via Zoom throughout a pandemic.

As soon as the words, 'The meeting has been ended by the host' appear on my screen, my smile fades. Summer always joked that I have a bad case of RBF—resting bitch face. It used to bother me because well . . . who wants to have that, but now that I've been teaching for a few years, any break from a smile brings me relief. Not wanting the interview committee to see my RBF, I do a quick check to ensure I'm logged off the call and close my laptop before completely abandoning my fake smile. Leaning back in my chair, my eyelids meet for a moment to rest. Within an instant, I see Summer's face. *Ugh, I miss her so freaking much. It's so unfair,* I think to myself.

I decide to distract myself, so I grab my phone and shoot off a text to my old high school best friends, Mason and Natalie.

ME

Got the job.

MASON

Yes, queen! We get to work together. SO EXCITED!!!

NATALIE

Knew you could do it, A. Looking forward to hanging out again like old times.

I'M SO happy to spend more time with them again. Mason went away to college but moved back to teach in Lake View, and Natalie joined the army right out of high school. After serving six years, she ended up back in our hometown, too. Apparently now it's my turn to go back there as well, too. Don't get me wrong, getting to be closer to mom and dad—and Mason and Natalie—will be great. And the idea of teaching with Mason is giving me some strength to follow through with another year of it, despite how it affected my mental health over the past couple years. I just . . . despise change. I thrive with order, routine, and structure.

I like to think that maybe it won't be so bad with Mason working there. He's someone I can depend on as both a friend and coworker. Coworkers, especially teachers, can be the 'make it or break it' for a school. But now that I think about it, I'm fairly certain Samantha Leeman, our high school's cheer captain who was annoying as hell, teaches there, too. I hope she's not on the fifth grade team with me.

I stand up and make my way to the bathroom. The mirror reflects that I'm flushed from the interview, so I turn on the faucet to splash water on my face. The coolness of the water wakes and calms me at once. Grabbing the beautiful hand towel I've cared too much about, I dry my face. I stare at my reflection in the mirror. The white surrounding my green eyes is turning bloodshot. I tuck a strand of my hair behind my ear, allowing a deep breath to exit through my nostrils. Thoughts invade my mind again. Can I really keep teaching? My work-life balance these past five years has been, well . . . nonexistent. It's quite tiresome to feel like you put so much time and effort into something, and yet still feel like it's not enough. It is never enough. Teaching has drained my cup, but now that I'm about to be living at my parents' beach house in my hometown, I figure what better time than now to give teaching a second chance. Summer would've wanted me to. She and I always played "school" when we were kids, and I can't remember a time when I wasn't the teacher. If only it were as simple and fun of a job as kid-Autumn imagined.

It's not just teaching I'm burnt out from. Ever since my first year of college, a little over a decade ago, I'll admit I've been going through the motions. The motions everyone is encouraged and supposed to go through. The norms. Societal expectations. I graduated high school, attended college, got married, and bought a two-story house with, quite literally, a white picket fence. To those on the outside looking in, my life couldn't be more "perfect." To me though, it has been far from it. I glance around my house, possibly for the last time. My breath slows for a minute as I take it all in. I close my eyes and think about all this house

—this life, really—and all it has provided to me. The thing I hate to admit the most is how scared I am with all this change. I don't like taking risks and I sure as hell hate unpredictability. Now that change has forced itself on me, I at least want to feel in control of some of it. The punches keep on rolling in, but I won't allow them to continue to do so. Not anymore. I need to plan and get things back under control.

My eyes open, and I reach for my laptop again. I've got to get out of Greenwich and book a flight back home. Now that the divorce is finalized, it's time to restart my life and give teaching a second chance.

WELL, tonight is already Meet the Teacher Night. Never in a million years did I think I'd be entering the doors of Lake View Elementary again, yet here I am walking into the all too familiar building. Tears flood my eyes. I thought I could do this, but maybe not. Now with Summer gone, both the season and my sister, I feel like I'm holding on by a thread.

I grab the door handle to Room 161. Next to the room number, I see a faint marking on a yellow post-it note which reads "Ms. Parker." I'm still adjusting to the fact that I'm no longer Mrs. Cunningham. Will I even recognize my own name when the students say it? *Get it together, Autumn. You'll be fine.*

A voice from behind me shouts, "Autumn—oh my god, is that really you?"

I shudder. I recognize that voice. It's Samantha Leeman. I haven't seen her since high school, but I would recognize that screechy voice of hers anywhere. She was the girl who always acted like we were friends, but then went after all the guys I liked. I think she and Zayn were together before he and I dated, but I can't remember for sure.

I turn around, hoping she doesn't notice my forced politeness. "Hi, Sam. Yep, it's really me."

"I seriously cannot wait to work with you. How exciting is this? It'll be just like old times!" she screeches.

I scan her features. Given that it's been over a decade since I last saw her, I must admit she hasn't changed a bit. I lie, "Yeah, it's going to be so great."

"You excited about the new school year?" she asks.

I exhale. "I think so. Just a little nervous."

"Me too. Always the back-to-school jitters." Samantha points as she walks over to the classroom across from mine. "Well, let me know if you need anything, teaching bestie. I'm just right across the hall." Not sure if I'm cringing more at the fact that she's directly across from me or at her use of the word "bestie."

I nod with a smile as I remind myself that as much as I dread change, I'm excited about the possibilities of a new school year. I still don't know if teaching is for me. These past years have been nothing but hard, but one thing I know for sure is that it always puts a smile on my face to get to see and meet my students. Just like any toxic marriage, that's really all that keeps me being hopeful and hanging on—the kids.

My classroom door closes behind me, and I can already hear chatter down the hall. I make sure the room is still set up and turn on my laptop and projector before Meet the Teacher Night officially begins.

When I prop open the classroom door, a family is already right there waiting to enter. The minute I see the adorable little girl with them, I can't help but smile.

"Hi there, welcome in! I'm Ms. Cu—oops, sorry." I shake my head and chuckle. "I'm Ms. Parker. What's your name?"

"Mikayla. Are you a new teacher here?" she asks, her large brown eyes looking at me inquisitively.

I laugh before responding, "Well, it's more like a yes and no. I haven't taught here yet, but I was a student here when I was your age. Since this was my elementary school too, this feels like home."

Mikayla's grin widens, introducing me to her neon pink braces. They make her even cuter. "That's awesome!" She exclaims.

I see a line forming behind her, which urges me to end the conversation so others can come in. "Well, come on in and make yourselves comfortable. There are some pages of information at the table over there, and then you're free to take a seat anywhere you like."

I stand near the door with my welcoming smile as more students and parents file in. In the most natural way, my shoulders drop, and my jaw unclenches. I can feel the anxiety fade more with every student who enters, bringing a little more comfort and familiarity to my heart. My cheeks are warm from the adrenaline.

Another family approaches me with a question about riding the bus. I don't know a thing about the bus transportation routes and routines, so I say, "You know what, I'm not really sure, but let me write that down on a sticky note so I remember to find out for you."

I make my way closer to the table on the opposite side of the room where I've stored post-it notes and pens. The family follows me, so I try to keep a reasonable pace. When I arrive at the table, I grab a pen from my favorite hedgehog coffee mug and jot down the reminder. I look up, letting them know I'll be in touch with them as soon as

I find out more information. My watch buzzes, alerting me of a phone call from a number I don't have saved. I quickly hit the button to silence the notification, returning my focus back to the family. They thank me a couple more times when my gaze flickers to the familiar figure at the door. My body tenses and butterflies fill my stomach.

There he is—my first love. The first guy to ever break my heart.

Zayn Mitchell.

His eyes meet mine. Here he is, standing in my class-room with a shirt tight enough in the arms to showcase ripped biceps and pearly white smile that hasn't changed since I've last seen him over a decade ago. The scruff on his chin makes me wonder how it'd feel to kiss him now. Liam has always been clean-shaven, so I wonder if scruff would bother me or if I'd like it better. My heart stops beating for a second. *Get it together, Autumn.*

The realization sets in. Zayn is here. At *my* Meet the Teacher Night. The audacity of this guy.

Ugh. Damn it. What is he even doing here? My face flushes and my body trembles. I feel weak, and not just in my knees, but all over my entire body. *Autumn, breathe. Quit being so nervous. Just approach him already and kick his butt outta here!*

I wade through the sea of people entering my class-room, faking smiles and politely saying, "Excuse me." Confusion cuts through the room as parents wander around in search of their child's new teacher. But my focus remains on getting over to Zayn. I have to know why he's here right now and let him know—however obvious it might feel to me—that he shouldn't be here right now.

His smile grows larger as I approach, but my blood starts to boil more the closer I get. I cross my arms, staring at him for a second. He doesn't say a word, just keeps showing off those ridiculously perfect teeth.

"Um . . . hi," I say. My hand makes its way to my hip.

"Hello, Ms. Parker," he playfully responds by adding emphasis on my maiden name.

The familiarity of his voice heats my body, a mixture of nerves and rage all rolled into one. "Oh my God," are the only words I'm able to spew from my mouth.

He laughs. "Nope. Not God. Zayn, remember?"

I scoff and slightly roll my eyes on the outside, but inside, my heart thumps loudly. It's so loud I can hear it pounding in my ears. *Oh no! Can he hear it?* My face flushes more.

As that perfect grin of his grows wider, I can't help but smile back. *No, do not smile at this jerk.* My mouth doesn't want to listen though. Years ago, he ended things without a true explanation. Well, a lousy excuse, in my opinion, anyway. One minute we were in love and ready to ride out our four-year plan of attending college and living together. The next, he decided to stay here. In this godforsaken town. Going against the plans we made together. No further contact. Nothing. More than anything, I still want to be upset with him—maybe throw something at him or just run away—but I'm pretty sure the parents here would not be impressed to see their child's new teacher do either of those things. What could he possibly be doing here?

"Well, Autumn—err, Ms. Parker—you look . . . amazing. Good to see you after all this time." He clears his throat while loosening the inside of his collar as if wearing an imaginary tie. "How are you?" he asks in his smooth, deep voice. I could listen to it all day. Even after all this time, it's so comfortable to me, like hearing an old song you once loved playing on the radio.

My mouth opens, but not a single word exits. Instead, a

million questions flood my mind—*What is he doing standing here, on such an important night for me? Did he seriously come here to see me after all this time? To what—talk things over?*

Moments pass that feel like forever until I finally stumble upon some words, "I'm, uh . . . fine."

"Fine? Hmph." He pauses for a moment, then offers, "Well, I wanted to offer my condolences. I'm so sorry to hear about Summer. And look, I'm here if you need anything. Truly."

I hurriedly respond with "I appreciate it." I release a small sigh, pausing to think of how to say goodbye. My chest rises as I take a deep breath. "Well, thanks so much for coming by, but it's probably best for you to leave now. I'd like to make a good first impression to my new class and their parents." I give him a stern look before leaning in to quietly tell him, "We can always chat and reconnect later, but not *now*. This is totally inappropriate." I want to inch away from him, but the woodsy scent of his cologne has me lingering.

His eyebrows raise. "I'm sorry, Autumn, but I can't just leave . . ." He wraps his arm around a young, lanky girl with bangs. A student. I stare blankly trying to comprehend. "Ms. Parker, I'd like you to meet Riley." He gestures to the girl. She looks just like him. "My big fifth grader," he says, squeezing at her side. "She's gonna be in your class this year."

Wait, what?! He has a daughter? Shit. He's got a little family now, which means he's probably happily married. Not that I'm wishing otherwise. Good for him. It's been almost twelve damn years for crying out loud. My eyes betray me as they travel to his left hand. No ring. When I glance back up at him, he shakes his head and smirks. At this point, Riley might call me Ms. Tomato-Faced Parker.

I quickly gain composure enough to say, "Hi, Riley, it's

so nice to meet you. Welcome! Are you excited for fifth grade?"

"Yes, I can't wait to be in your class!" Riley exclaims with a big, sweet grin showing off a glowing smile that looks just like Zayn's. I smile genuinely as I take a longer look at her. She certainly has her father's big, dark eyes, too.

"Excuse me—are you Ms. Parker?" an unfamiliar voice interrupts my thoughts. *Shit.* It's still Meet the Teacher Night. *Snap out of it, Autumn. You're still at work.*

Without taking my eyes off Riley, I answer, "Yes, that's me."

I slowly turn to face the woman asking while I exchange one final glance with Zayn. His lips form an understanding smile, and he takes his daughter to find a seat.

This woman is asking me questions about the school year and telling me all about her son, but I'm still processing that Zayn is here. With his *daughter*. Who will be my student this year.

I pretend to glance at my watch and politely explain, "Well, it's been a pleasure to meet you, but you must excuse me as it's actually time for the presentation to begin. I'm looking forward to having William in my class this year."

I start to head up to the front of the room. Sweat beads in almost every crevice of my body. My chest tightens, and my throat feels as though it's closing in on itself. *You can do this. Keep breathing.* I take the reminder seriously and let out a few deep breaths. Focusing on breathing is a technique that often does help when the anxiety hits. *God, please don't let me have a panic attack right now.* The room starts to spin as I approach the projector, just focusing on getting to the front of the room.

I turn to face the crowded room of parents, future students, and Zayn with his lovely daughter.

I put on my classroom microphone, ensure my laptop is in presentation mode, and I begin.

"Hi, everyone. Welcome to Meet the Teacher Night."

3
☑ Take a Four Horsemen Shot

The door closes behind me and it feels good to be back in an old familiar place—Karma Cafe. For as long as the town can remember, this local cafe has been a full-blown bar at night—a constant in an ever-changing place. I could really use a drink after searching the entire beach house for mine and Summer's WOLO list. I thought for sure we'd kept it there so we could check some of the items off whenever we spent time together. The notebook is there, but the list isn't. Maybe Summer ripped it out and did the items without me? I think she had already done at least half that list before she passed. She wasn't afraid of anything. Now that she's gone, it's my turn. And what better way to start than with some liquid courage?

"Hey there, Autumn. Long time, no see," Joe, the bartender, greets me.

I do a quick glance around before hanging my crossbody on the back of the barstool and taking a seat. "Hey Joe."

Joe is in his mid-forties now, at least, with more gray than brown in his hair and mustache. He's a short, scruffy guy, who despite his intimidating looks, always has a smile on his face. I notice the dark circles under his eyes though.

"I'm so sorry about Summer. I sure miss her around here. How ya holding up?" he asks.

"Thanks. Uh, could be better. But I'm alright, I guess."

He nods in understanding before grabbing the bottle of Tito's. He remembers my drink. "Want the usual?" he asks.

I take another look around noticing couples all around me engaged in conversation. "Yeah, that'd be gre—"

"Wait a minute, Missy. You know what, I've got 'just the thing' for ya."

I hesitate but give a thumbs up to be polite. I watch as he begins concocting some type of cocktail for me, hoping it's something I'll actually enjoy. I shoot off a text to Mason and Natalie while I wait.

ME

Hey, I'm at Karma. You guys coming out tonight or what? I'm ready for some drinks after quite the Meet the Teacher Night.

I shove my phone back into my bag as Joe sets down a cocktail I've never seen before right in front of me. "What is this?" I ask.

He grins before he answers with, "I call it the 'No Regrets.' And you look like you're regretting too much shit right now."

Am I regretting this move? Or regretting going back to teach-ing? Regretting . . . everything?

Joe clears his throat to interrupt my thinking. He's still waiting for me to take a sip, so I finally do. The taste is sweet, but not unbearably so. I only know there is alcohol in it by the warmth that fills my throat. "Oh my God, Joe, that's truly one of the best things I've tasted in years. I gotta know what's in it," I say, genuinely curious since I've never tasted anything even close to how delicious this drink is.

"Nah, bartenders' word to not share secret recipes. But I do gotta ask, any regrets?" He pauses for a minute before adding on to his question "Err—with the drink?"

"No, sir. You've truly outdone yourself and managed to surprise me. I appreciate it."

"How'd my man Joe surprise you?" A familiar voice chimes in. I look at the stool next to me and find Kayla, an old friend of mine who I haven't seen in years.

Kayla takes a seat next to me. "Hey girl hey," she says in her sweet-but-sassy voice. She offers me a side hug.

"Hey hey," I say. "Good to see you, girl. How have you been?"

She waves her hand. "Oh, I'm doing just fine. I'm so sorry about Summer."

"Thank you," I say, getting numb from the number of condolences I've received in the past couple of days.

"So, how long you in town for?"

"Umm, well about that. I'm moving back."

"Ahh, I'm so excited to hear this! I've missed you so much over the past few years. Lake View just ain't the same without ya, girl."

My phone vibrates the chair. "Oh, wait, I think Mason and Natalie are texting me," I tell Kayla.

"Ooh, tell them to come! I haven't seen them in a few months, believe it or not," she replies.

I unlock my phone with the scan of my face and swipe open my messages app.

NATALIE

Girl, I don't think I can make it after all. You and Mace have fun!

MASON

Autumn, I can't make it out tonight. Still at school. FML.

I glance back at Kayla with a sigh. "Well, Mason and Nat can't make it out tonight after all."

"Oh babe, what a bummer," Kayla offers. She waves her hand in front of her playfully. "Don't worry, though. You got me tonight."

I smile, feeling comfort that I at least have one friend here. The bar door swings open, and a warmth takes over my body as I awkwardly stare at the man who enters. Zayn. I place my focus back on Kayla before he notices me too. *Really? Twice in one day?* I ask myself.

"Oh boy," Kayla says.

I blink. "What?"

"You look like you've just seen a ghost. Don't ya remember how small this town is?"

I laugh. "Oh, trust me, I'm remembering very quickly."

Kayla giggles just as Joe asks her what she'd like to drink. She points to mine, "Um, I think I want one of those. Looks delish."

"You got it, Kayla. You won't regret it—get it?" he jokes.

Kayla rolls her eyes at him. Their banter makes me realize it's not all bad being back home.

Joe clears his throat and points to my near-empty glass. "Want another?"

I contemplate saying yes for a moment, but then it hits me. The WOLO list had a drink on it. "Actually, can I get a Four Horsemen shot this time?"

"A what?" Kayla asks with such dramatic emphasis, as though I just asked to do a body shot off of Joe.

"You sure about that one, little miss? Those are pretty rough," Joe explains. "I also can't offer a No Regrets disclaimer with that one."

I laugh. "That's fair, but I'm sure. Thanks, Joe," I say with a fake confidence knowing damn well I can't handle liquor like that.

He offers a quick nod in agreement before making it.

Kayla looks at me, "Wait what . . . a Four Horsemen? What the hell is that?"

"It's this drink Summer and I used to think was so badass, but we always chickened out before taking it. It's a shot with equal parts of the four J names: Jim Beam, John Jameson, Johnnie Walker, and Jack Daniels."

Kayla's jaw drops dramatically. "Seriously?"

"Seriously," I say.

After Joe drops off my Four Horsemen shot and Kayla's 'No Regrets,' she raises her glass and says, "To us, Autumn. And to a great, unexpected girls' night."

Before I'm able to lift mine to meet hers, she drops her drink back down to the table. "Oh my God, you'll never guess who's heading over to you right now."

I scoff. "Please tell me he's not. Aside from us discussing his daughter's progress in class, I really don't have anything to say to him."

"Wait, Riley is in your class this year?" she asks.

I nod before looking down at the giant shot in my hands.

"Oof. Well, that's gonna be pretty awkward, for sure," she says.

I wave my hand as if it's no big deal, when in fact, my heartbeat completely disagrees. The very thought of him coming up to me is turning my stomach into a butterfly garden and sending my heart into a fistfight with my chest.

My head slowly turns as I pretend to flip my hair over my shoulder. I spot him in my peripherals. Wait—do I want him to talk to me? What could he possibly want to talk about? By the time I allow my head to complete the full turn, I catch him walking right past Kayla and me. With his back facing me now, I give my eyes permission to watch him. I watch as he strikes up a chat with the one and only DJ, who's been hosting open mic and karaoke nights here for at least the past fifteen years. Maybe they're good friends now. Not that it's any of my business. I look back at Kayla, trying to force myself back to our conversation before Zayn rudely interrupted. Not to his knowledge, of course.

"Oh, never mind," Kayla says. "I guess he isn't coming over after all."

I sigh with relief. "Thank God," I say. "Okay, now where were we?"

She smirks before raising her glass to me again. "Cheers, babe."

"Yes, cheers." Our glasses clink, we set them down, and I swig back what's probably the strongest, most painful shot of my adult life. The burning sensation flows down my throat and I cringe as if I just ate a whole lemon.

"Was it as bad as it looks?"

I grit my teeth and nod several times. I search for a chaser and quickly signal to Joe for some water. He laughs as he pours me a glass.

When the glass of water is in front of me, I push the straw to the side and act as though it's a new shot with how fast I chug it.

"Note to self: do not take a Four Horsemen shot," Kayla says.

My eyes squint from disgust at the thought of the drink again. "Girl, never again. I'm not even really much of a drinker except for Tito's or the occasional glass of red."

Kayla slowly sips her No Regrets, nodding along. She sets it down. "I get that. I'm starting to slow down myself, to be honest. Our thirties are right around the corner and all this drinking I've been doing over the course of my twenties is bound to catch up with me."

"True that," I say, reflecting on how my twenties have been pretty boring until now.

"So, where are you gonna be staying now that you're back?" Kayla asks.

"At my parents' beach house, actually. They've been fixing it up the past couple of years and were about to sell it. But now that plan has changed since I've decided to move back for a while."

"Just a while?"

"Yeah," I shrug. "I don't really have a plan right now. For the first time in my life. And now without Summer, I feel even more stuck."

Kayla extends her hand to my shoulder. "I can't even imagine what it's like for you. I have to tell you, the entire town ain't been the same without Summer. She was so much fun and loved by everyone."

A tear makes its way down my cheek. "Joe, I'm ready for another drink," I yell to him.

"Another Four Horsemen?" he asks.

"Absolutely not," I say, trying not to think about how drunk I probably am from the first one. "I'll do a Tito's and soda with a lime this time, please."

He nods. "Back to the usual. There's the Autumn I remember."

Kayla laughs at Joe's remark. "That's the Autumn I remember, too. You would've never taken a sip of anything that dangerous the last time I saw you. Although it has been at least what—four years or so?"

"Yup, you're right," I admit with a chuckle. "I know it sounds ridiculous, but I'm trying to honor Summer by completing this bucket list we made together years ago. I've searched the beach house already. Since I've had no luck finding the dang thing, I'm trying to remember what was on it. And 'Take a Four Horsemen shot' was one of the things I do remember."

"Oh! How fun! I love that. So, what else do you remember is on the list?"

I smirk at her. *Maybe this night doesn't have to end terribly.* "Dance on a bar . . ."

Kayla downs her drink before hollering to Joe. "Two more, Joe! And keep 'em coming!"

4
☑ Dance On a Bar

The sound of Bon Jovi's "Livin' on a Prayer" reverberates throughout the bar while a man in his early forties screams into the karaoke mic.

"Come on girl, you ready or what?" Kayla asks me.

"Don't get me wrong, I want to do the things on the list, but I'm not sure I'm ready to tackle this one yet," I admit.

Kayla looks around. "If you don't want to do this, that's fine. We don't have to."

"Thanks, maybe one more drink will help me," I say. She nods and we take our seats. Zayn is seated on the opposite side of the bar now, with his old friend Ryker right next to him. I can't help but keep looking in their direction. Ryker notices and gives me a wink. He and Zayn were always the best of friends, and it does make me happy to know that nothing has changed between the two of them.

I wave, which feels a bit awkward. Zayn looks directly at me now and gives a nod. My already-flushed cheeks get hotter.

"Babe, you okay?" Kayla asks, interrupting this little moment.

My eyes shift back to her. "Shit, yes. Just being my awkward self, I guess."

She grabs my shoulders and gets closer to me. "Listen,

Autumn, forget Zayn and forget that you're back in this dump. Let's just let loose and focus on having fun."

"You're right." I signal Joe over for one more drink.

His eyebrows raise before he says, "You sure? Who's driving?"

"I'll have Mom come pick me up. She offered earlier, but I didn't realize I'd have this much to drink," I yell to him over the blaring music.

"Alright, as long as you're sure," he says, filling another glass with Tito's.

"Oh my God, Autumn," Kayla interjects. "Do you see that guy at the door?"

I turn my head to face the door. There's a guy who looks to be in his thirties, gelled-back blonde hair that reminds me a bit of Liam's. This guy is much taller though and looks like a southern boy from how he's dressed, a plain white shirt with distressed (from actual wear) jeans. Liam wouldn't be caught dead in such a thing.

"Oh, who is that?" I ask.

"Well, it's this guy, Callum. He and I went on a few dates and then he ghosted me. I don't know what the hell happened, but I was so into him," she explains.

"I can see why. He's really good looking," I say.

"Right?"

I shrug. "Maybe go chat with him?"

"No way. He needs to come to me. I'm done giving in to guys so easily." Kayla chugs the remainder of her drink as someone begins to sing, "Pour Some Sugar on Me," by Def Leppard.

"I don't blame you. You know what, Kayla? Screw these guys! Let's get our asses on the bar and have some fun."

I turn to my untouched vodka soda. Taking a deep breath, I grab it and use the tiny straw to drink as much as I can.

A stunned Kayla blinks several times at me. "What?" She yells. "It's so loud, but I could've sworn you said let's get on the bar?"

I finish off the drink before sliding the empty glass to the other side of the bar. I climb on the top of the stool and wave my hand up for Kayla.

She takes my hand and we both hop on the bar. I'm swaying my hips awkwardly as people hoot and holler from below us. Kayla's hands make her way up and down her body, and I'd swear she's a coyote from the movie *Coyote Ugly* with how well she's dancing.

She makes her way closer to me, starting to grind on me as the guy sings, "I'm hot, sticky sweet, from my head to my feet, yeah."

We grab hands in the air and both start lowering ourselves to the bar. I allow my hips and butt to be the first to come back up. I watch as Kayla releases my hands and turns around to keep dancing and walking along the bar. I follow her lead and do the same.

Images start to blur around me, and I feel hands grabbing at my bare ankles right above my wedges. I don't let them stop me. *I feel good.* Eyes closed, I allow my hips to shake from side to side. My arms flail above me, and I let my hands slowly make their way through my hair, trying to act sexy like Kayla.

"Over here, baby!" A man hollers above the music. My eyes open to find a much older man. His hand takes hold of my ankle as he tries to pull me down to his level.

"Back off," I yell down to him, trying to escape his grasp. Taking a step further, my ankle is set free, and I lose my balance on the skinny bar. My entire backside meets the sticky bar floor.

"Owwww," I yell out, prying open my eyes to a bunch of blurry faces.

"Autumn . . ." I hear Kayla ask me if I'm okay, but I can't make out which face is hers above me. My whole body hurts and my head throbs. My right foot swells with pain.

"Everyone, please step aside," says a familiar voice that snaps me back to reality. The same deep voice continues to say, "Don't worry, I'll get her to the hospital."

A woman screams, "There's blood on the floor!"

Blood? From where? Who's bleeding? Me? I touch my head and feel moisture. Slowly bringing my hand down to see it, my hand refuses to steady. My vision remans blurry.

A moment later, my whole body seems to be moving too, almost as though I'm flying. *Am I dying?* I'm not ready to die when I've just been slightly elevating from the rock bottom of my life. Wait—nope, now I feel something different. Feels like I'm flying in a good way, not a dying way. Butterflies fill my stomach. Goosebumps form on my arms. That can only mean one thing . . . Zayn must be carrying me. I mean seriously, could this get any more embarrassing?

As I continue to gain awareness, I manage to scream, "Put me down!" right as we reach the door to the parking lot. "Zayn, this is absolutely ridiculous!" I try to squirm out of his hold. I continue to try a few more times but to no avail. He gets annoyed with my unsuccessful attempts and lowers me from his shoulder to his chest. He holds me like his new bride, as if we're about to enter a honeymoon suite. I guess it really can get more embarrassing.

My head feels as though someone is pounding on it with a hammer. I open my eyes to check if my vision is any better, but I try not to look directly at Zayn, so I look around at the parking lot instead. I can see that there are cars, but they're more like colorful lumps in a row. They aren't all just lumps though. I swear I recognize his old, beat-up Ford truck.

He fumbles to get his key out of his back pocket while still managing to carry me. Finally getting the key, he opens the passenger door and sets me down on the seat. He pauses for a moment. My vision improves enough to let me stare into those delicious, dark chocolate eyes of his. Everything around us remains a blur, but now I'm not sure if it's just from my fall. My heart beats so loudly it sounds as though someone is playing the drums in the backseat. It could be my head pounding though, too. Yeah, let's go with that.

"Uh, sorry, excuse me . . ." he says reaching underneath me to lower the seat. My body jolts back. His hand grazes my leg, and I feel like I'm on fire. I'm now lying down in the seat and feeling a sense of deja vu to losing my virginity in this very truck. I know most people typically regret their first time, but mine was unregrettable—*wait, is that even a word? I don't think so.* The pounding in my head brings me back to the present.

My eyes make his way to his lips like a magnet, and I can't help but wonder what he tastes like now. He notices my stare. I panic and interrupt our moment by saying, "You know, I just got divorced." *What the hell, Autumn? Really?*

"Autumn, your head is bleeding from a terrible fall back there at the bar. All I'm gonna do is make sure you're okay. I'm taking you to the hospital now. Nothing else."

I almost laugh, but my head throbs in agreement with him.

"Okay," I say, "well, thank you for making sure I'm fine. You really don't have to worry about me though, Zayn."

His eyebrows raise, and he lets out a sigh. I swear I hear him whisper, "I never stopped."

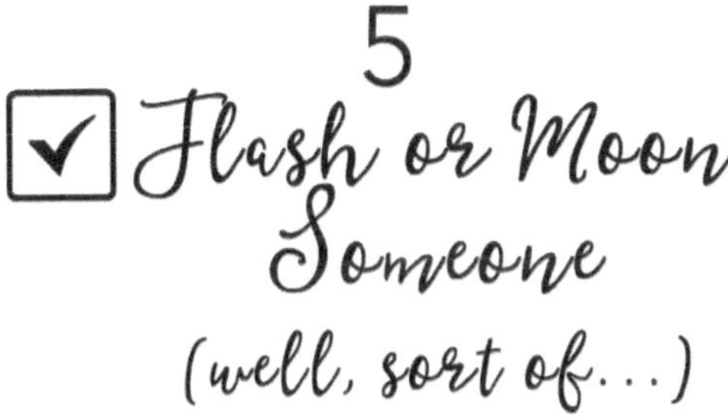

"Oh, honey! You're awake! How are you feeling?" my mom asks. "Your dad was just here a bit ago, but since you were sleeping, he went over to the house to let Max out.

"I'm okay," I answer quickly before adding, "My brain doesn't feel so foggy anymore, but I'm still tired."

"What happened? The nurses told me you were dancing on a bar. That doesn't sound like you," Mom says.

My head throbs. I debate telling her about the WOLO list but decide against it for now. "I know. I was trying to loosen up, I guess."

"Well thank goodness you're alright. The doc says you've fractured your foot. They're also wanting to monitor you for a possible concussion since you threw up so much . . . but it could be from all the alcohol, too." Her judgment punctures me like a wound.

"Yeah, I went a little too hard tonight," I admit.

She blows out a breath. "Well, you just got back home. And you know I worry. So, let's take it easy on your dear old mom, will ya?"

"I'm sorry, Mom. Trust me, it won't happen again." I search around the room.

"Oh, before I forget, I let Natalie and Mason know you were okay. They were both blowing up your phone asking how you were doing, so I called Natalie and gave her an update," she says.

"I bet they both show up today. Can you send a text telling them I promise I'm fine and they don't need to bother coming?" I ask.

"I told Natalie that you were resting. It's very early in the morning. She said she and Mason will try to come by a little later in the day."

I nod, appreciating that response. I'm not sure why I'm fighting having visitors, especially my friends. I was super sick with pneumonia a few years ago while living in Greenwich. Ended up in the hospital there. And other than Liam (and eventually Summer and Mom and Dad), none of my so-called friends showed up for me. Maybe I'm afraid the only person who would show up for me is now gone forever.

I know I shouldn't care, but I feel weird that Zayn didn't stick around. Although, why on earth was I expecting him to?

"Did Zayn . . .? Never mind." My eyes close, and I wave my hand ever so slightly from the bed since my body still aching.

Mom grabs my hand in comfort. I open my eyes to see a smile on her face. "Zayn is doing okay. Thank God he was sober enough to bring you here. That was very sweet of him to be there for you."

I scoff. "Mhmm. Well, and I'm sure you've already heard that his daughter will be in my class this year, huh?"

"I did. You know how fast news travels around here. In his defense, the chance of that happening was high—with Lake View Elementary being the only elementary school around here."

A sigh escapes me. "I know, Mom," I say feeling like no

one understands why I'm so upset that I now have to regularly see the guy who broke my heart.

"Listen honey, I know you think that what he did back in high school is unforgivable, but maybe now that you're back here, he'll start to grow on you again. Especially now, with the divorce and everything. You might get lonely is all."

Even with my mouth agape, I struggle to find a response to that. "Really, Mom?"

"Oh, don't start acting like an upset teenager. You know what I meant. I just want you to find love and be happy, my sweet girl." My mom turns and takes a seat in the one chair in the room.

I guess I really am sounding like a teenager. I don't know why I let him crawl under my skin so much. It feels like a lifetime ago after all. "No need to worry about that. I am happy, and I don't need to be in love with some guy in order for that to happen. Honestly, I know I always wanted what you and Dad had, but now that the shit hit the fan with Liam, I'm thinking I'll be better off alone," I admit out loud for the first time.

My mom nods her head. "You're right, I'll leave it alone. I know you're still grieving the divorce, and I promise to let you have your alone time." She takes a deep breath. "Before I forget, I know you had asked about Zayn, and I wanted to tell you, he's—" My mom is interrupted from the opening of the door. We both watch in awe as two nurses wheel Zayn in on a travel gurney. He looks over at me and the side of his mouth turns up in an attempted smile. *Unbelievable!*

The nurses set Zayn up in the bed next to mine, with only a curtain dividing us. Dr. Scout makes his way over to me. "What the hell is he doing in here?" I ask loud enough so the whole room hears me. I direct my attention towards my mom. "And you! Mom, you told me he left."

"No, I didn't. I was letting you know that he was alright. I didn't have the chance to tell you he was still here, but as a patient. He apparently fainted while you were getting your IV set up."

You've got to be kidding me.

Zayn glances over at me as a nurse continues to get him set up. He mouths an apology.

One of the nurses chimes in, "Mr. Mitchell requested that he just be placed in this room so he could make sure you were alright. And I definitely owe him one since he helped save my niece's cat from a tree last week." *Pfft, big deal.*

Another nurse chimes in, "I don't know what we'd do without Mr. Mitchell around here." The other nurses swoon and look over at Zayn with looks of gratitude and pining. I can't help but roll my eyes.

"Oh, how diplomatic," I say, allowing the sarcasm to come out unfiltered.

I CAN'T BELIEVE my high school ex-boyfriend is sharing a hospital room with me right now. The nurse left the dividing curtain open while I was asleep. But now I've been awake for what feels like eternity, and we haven't spoken a word to each other. I genuinely don't know whether I want to yell, scream, or cry at Zayn—or just continuing with this deafening silence. Before I can decide, Zayn breaks it by saying, "Aw come on, Autumn. You really aren't going to say a word to me the whole night? We're trapped in here together so we may as well make the best of it."

I scoff. "You know, I knew I'd run into you, but I've been back in town for less than a week, and you keep seeming to end up where I am."

"I respect that you probably had no intention of seeing me—not this soon anyway—but how was I supposed to know you'd end up teaching my ten-year-old this year?" Zayn gives an innocent shrug.

I hold my focus to the chair in the room, where my mom sat before. When it breaks, I decide to look directly at him, but he pretends not to notice.

I clear my throat. "OK, fine. I'll admit that having your daughter in my class this school year is total coincidence, but you shouldn't be here in a hospital bed next to me right now. Always having to steal my thunder . . ." I roll my eyes, knowing how much he used to hate that.

"Just one bone. My foot." I shake my head.

"Actually, it was one of your phalanges."

I scoff. "And what are you some kind of . . . doctor now? Or a vet since you're apparently rescuing cats."

He chuckles and shakes his head. "Nope, I'm a firefighter."

"*Of course* you are," I snap.

We sit back in silence for a moment before I say, "I guess I do owe you a thank you."

"Okay, now we're getting somewhere. It may not be the most meaningful apology I've received, but you know what? I'll take it." Zayn attempts to lift himself a bit more with the excitement of engaging in conversation with me. "You know, come to think of it, it's more believable that you did this on purpose."

"What—you've got to be kidding me," I say, wishing I could cross my arms.

Zayn smirks.

"Okay, Mr. Mitchell, so let me get this new theory of yours straight. You think I fell from the bar on purpose?"

"You tell me, Miss Parker," he says. I note the switch from Ms. to Miss.

"I think it'd be more likely I'd fake my death to get out of a conversation with you," I respond.

"Ouch!" Zayn says as he playfully covers his heart with his hand. I can't help but smile at such a dorky move.

"Oh please," I say.

He flashes me a smile that makes me melt. *Ugh, no! Do not fall for his stupid good looks again.* I look over at my heart rate level on the monitor, saying a quick prayer it won't increase so quickly, somehow possibly triggering an alarm for a nurse to come in right now. Physically, I'm beginning to feel fine. Emotionally, not so much.

"Autumn," Zayn says with obvious hesitation.

"Yes?"

"Never mind," he says, waving his hand in the air.

"Don't back track now. Spit it out."

He sighs heavily before saying, "I know it's going to take a lot for you to forgive me, but I'd really like to try to be friends. I mean you're back here, and Riley is in your class . . . it just seems like a good time to make amends."

I briefly weigh the options in my mind. "I guess you have a point. I don't know about friends . . . but we can at least try to get along for this school year. For Riley's sake," I offer.

He nods. "I promise to make things better between us."

A part of me really wants to trust this is true, but I know he doesn't usually follow through with his promises, which leads me to ask, "How come you never told me you had a daughter? And a ten-year-old one at that?"

"It's not like I've had many chances to before now. You

and I haven't exactly kept in touch. I'm not on any social media or anything. And after graduation, when I . . . stayed behind, I got a bit reckless, I guess you could say." He shrugs. "It all worked out, though, since my little Riley bug is honestly the best thing that's ever happened to me."

Reckless? Not sure if I'm jealous or angry at his admission. I decide to keep the focus on Riley. "I can tell," I say genuinely. "You seem like you're a good dad, Zayn."

I debate asking who Riley's mom is. I wonder if I know her. Instead, I reach for the cup of water the nurse left for me on the table, but my arms aren't long enough.

"Sorry I can't be of much assistance. Do you want me to call the nurse?" Zayn asks.

"I can do it myself," I say. "I just need to scoot up a little bit more—ugh, screw it. I'll just get up and get the damn cup myself."

I attempt to swing my legs over the side of the bed, but instead of successfully planting two feet on the ground, they slip out from underneath me. I fall to the ground with my backside facing Zayn.

"Ahhh!" I scream from utter embarrassment. An alarm goes off indicating I'm out of bed and unplugged from the machines.

"Shit, Autumn. You alright?" Zayn asks leaning forward in his bed.

I scoff. "I'm fine. How useless are these socks!" I gasp, feeling mortified. "Oh my gosh, wait a minute—can you see my butt?"

Zayn laughs out loud. "Well, now that you mention it, it does appear a full moon is out," he teases.

"Ahh! Quit looking at it!" I yell.

"Hey now, nothing I haven't seen before," he admits and laughs harder.

I squint in anger. "Ugh, so not funny!"

"You're right, sorry. Honestly, when we got here, I should've tied the gown for you," he offers.

I scoff, holding my torso up with one arm and turning my head to look at him. His eyes lock with mine for a moment as I try to figure out what to say or do.

Before I can reply, the door flies open. The nurses spot me on the floor and instantly rush to get me back into the bed. Once I'm settled, the nurse asks if there's anything else I need. I point to the water cup on the table.

The nurse hands it to me and I take the fastest sip I've ever taken. She starts to check my vitals and ensures I'm correctly hooked up to everything. When she finishes, she informs me that her name is Barb, and she'll be back again in a couple hours before the shift change.

Barb peeks over to Zayn and flashes him a smile. "Hey Mr. Mitchell, another nurse will be in shortly with your discharge paperwork. You doing okay for now?"

He shakes his head and tells her thank you. When Barb leaves the room, I burst into laughter.

Zayn looks over at me and asks, "What's so funny?"

I take a deep breath to control my laughter before replying, "It's Meet the Teacher Night, and instead of going out after to let loose, I'm now in a hospital bed with a possible concussion and a fractured foot lying next to my ex-boyfriend, who just saw my butt crack for the first time in almost twelve years."

"Well, when you put it that way, sounds like a pretty normal Meet the Teacher Night to me," he says in jest.

We both laugh for the next few minutes until our stomachs and cheeks hurt.

6

☑ Break a Bone

Opening my eyes, I realize I'm still in the hospital. The beeping from the machine sounds dull and steady. My headache has finally subsided. *Such a relief.* I glance over to check on Zayn, but he's not there. In fact, it's just me in the room. Alone. *Maybe mom does have a point . . . I've never really been alone.* I try to shake the thought away by thinking about my time with Zayn. My mom said he was a "changed man," and I secretly hope she's right. I still don't ever want to date him again. No more letting my heart get hurt.

Barb enters the room with another nurse. "Good morning, Autumn. How are you feeling this morning?"

"I'm actually feeling . . . well, more like myself. Maybe still a little tired, which I can't believe since I've slept so much," I admit.

"Oh yeah, that's a normal feeling. People tend to think otherwise, but believe or not, rest is actually much needed for potential concussions," she says as she types more information into the computer. "And what's your pain level at now?"

"I think it's safe to say a zero," I say. "Does this mean I can go back to work now? The school year has just started, and the first day is this Monday. I definitely need to plan."

"Oh honey, don't fret. You'll be back to work in no time." She continues typing briefly before scanning her badge a final time. She looks up and says, "Alright, my dear, this is goodbye from me. Tanya will be taking over as your nurse for the day shift."

Tanya flashes me a smile and says, "I'll be here if you need anything." She looks around the room, and then offers, "Can I get you any more water or ice?"

"Some more water would be great," I tell her.

"Sure thing," she says on her way out the door.

A few moments later, the door opens again, and I expect Tanya with my water. Instead, it's Zayn. My heart rate climbs a bit on the monitor. *Oof, please tell me he's not seeing that too.*

"What are you doing back here?" I ask him.

He moves closer to the bed, handing me a cup of water with one hand and clutching a couple of envelopes in the other.

"Sorry, um, yes. I haven't left yet. You were asleep when I got discharged, so I've been here waiting for you to wake up."

My chest floats up as I inhale. "Oh, why?" I ask.

"So, before I found out you were moving back here and assumed you were still with Liam. . ." Zayn pauses the moment I cringe at his mention of Liam's name. "Anyway, the whole point I'm trying to make is that Summer didn't think you'd ever move back here, but she knew you'd come to visit after she passed. For, like, the funeral and stuff. So, she gave me these two envelopes to give to you after she died."

I glare at him, trying to process what he's just said. "Wait, Summer gave *you* envelopes to give to *me?*" My voice squeaks from the shock.

"Yes, that's right," he says. "Look, I don't know why she chose me to give them to you, but she did. She didn't give a real reason, but as you know Summer, she was adamant with me that I make sure you received them after she died."

Tears reappear in my eyes again. Summer knew she was going to die, and then she left something—letters, I assume—in envelopes for me to read. I have some of my sister's last words right here in front of me. That she gave to my ex-boyfriend to give to me. At this point, I'm so relieved to have something more from her that it doesn't even matter why she made that choice. I'm simply happy she did.

"So, well, uh—here you go," Zayn says as he places them on the table next to me. Remembering the clumsy fumble I had last night, he moves the table directly over my lap for me to read them. "Alright, well that's pretty much it. I hope you get out soon." He starts to head for the door when he stops and says, "Autumn, I know we're still in some kind of gray area, but I'm here for you—no questions asked."He grabs the door handle.

"Wait," I say. *Autumn girl, what are you doing? Remember he's the jackass who broke your heart into a tiny million pieces. A relentless jackass at that.* Instead of yelling, I sigh. "Come sit." I motion towards a spot on my bed, not sure what the hell I'm doing right now. But what happened between us was ten years ago now. We've both clearly moved on.

"You sure?" he asks looking as equally puzzled as I feel.

I nod. "I mean, after all, Summer did give you them to give to me, so you may as well be here for support as I open them."

"Okay, sure," he says.

I pick up both envelopes. One is labeled with a note in Summer's handwriting that says, *Read me first. I mean it . . . open this one first.*

I chuckle a bit because even though it's writing, I can hear her voice scolding me to make sure I follow her directions. I sigh. "Okay, guess I'm opening this one first."

Inside the envelope, there are two pieces of paper. One

is not-so-new and looks like it was torn from a spiral note-book, but the other is just a plain piece of paper. I read the plain one first:

Dear Tum Tum,

I was never good with words, and I know you were, so don't judge me. By now you know I'm gone. I hope you threw me the best celebration of life there ever was because despite it ending so soon, my life was a pretty damn good one. I did live it to the fullest every day, and I can honestly say I have no regrets. I hope that one day when your time comes, you feel the same.

With that being said, in honor of my memory, and because I know you're a big scaredy cat who is afraid of change, I want you to complete our WOLO list. You may already have done a couple of things on it . . . like living your dream career, Miss Teacher, you! But, I KNOW for a fact there are several things on there that you haven't yet done. Don't be a chicken. For crying out loud, get buried in the sand by someone you trust. No one will leave you there to die (well, hope-fully not). Sushi and food trucks are delicious, and I promise you won't regret them.

Actually, looking through the list again, I don't think you'll regret ANY of them.

So, it's an order—finish the list. Go chase big dreams, take risks, and imagine I'm right there next to you every step of the way. Because you know what? I will be! My fabulous ghost self will be there cheering you on every time you cross an item off the list. You got this, sis.

I may no longer be living, but you still are. Remember that. We only live once . . . don't waste your life being too afraid to live.

Love you forever and always,
Summer

P.S. You cannot open the second envelope until the WOLO list is completed. I mean it.

The floodgates of my eyes release all at once, no tear gets left behind.

"Hey now, don't worry. It's all gonna be okay. Tissues?" Zayn says as he places a box of tissues down on the tray for me before extending his arm to meet mine for support.

I sob for several minutes. I'm past the expression of "ugly crying" right now. Zayn's hand leaves my arm to cup my face for a moment. His palm directs my chin, and it stops me a bit in my tracks. I pause as he wipes away my tears with his thumb. "It's all going to be okay, I promise."

Trust is the last thing he deserves from me right now, but I can't help but believe his words.

"I just . . . I miss her so much. She really is gone," I say through the sobs.

He guides me through several deep breaths, and I use some tissues to finally gain my composure back a bit.

"Thank you for the letters, and thank you for . . . you know, helping me," I say.

"Anytime," he says.

"Glad I already started working on it. She wants me to complete our WOLO list," I explain. "Which means . . ."

I open the second letter that was in the envelope, already knowing what it is—the WOLO list we created so many years ago.

"Wait, I'm sorry—the wo-what list?" he asks.

I let out a giggle. I forgot how silly it was. "The WOLO list," I clarify. "Do you remember when we graduated high school and there was that famous 'YOLO' song by Drake?"

He shakes his head. "Mhmm, that obnoxious one we heard for weeks on end, and everyone had those tee shirts . . . yeah, how could I forget?"

"Well, Summer had the idea that instead of 'You Only Live Once' we should make a bucket list, but since we were going to do it together, we'd call it 'WOLO' for 'We Only Live Once,'" I explain.

Zayn flashes me a smile, and it calms me even more. "Alright, I get it. So, let's see this list then."

I open the crumbled-up folded piece of now-yellowed notebook maper. Despite the couple of Diet Coke stains, it remains legible. Instantly, I'm brought back to that day where, even though my world had been turned upside down, Summer managed to cheer me up, as she always did.

Summer & Autumn's WOLO List:

1. Land your dream job:

Summer: travel blogger and photographer

Autumn: become a teacher

2. Eat sushi

3. Dance on a bar

4. Eat food from a food truck (for Autumn)

5. Take a Four Horsemen shot

6. Drive a jet ski

7. Get a tattoo

8. Be buried in the sand

9. Break a bone

10. Get high

11. Toilet paper Nick Hartzell's house

12. Go parasailing

13. Experience 100 mph in a car

14. Get a unique pet

15. Go on a blind date

16. Dance in a fountain

17. Ride a mechanical bull

18. Skinny-dip

19. Have sex on the beach

20. Go camping at Cherry Springs

21. Stay up and watch the sunrise

22. Throw a pie in Mr. Parson's (Summer's old retail manager's) face

23. Flash or moon someone

24. Crash a wedding
25. Take a class to learn something new
26. Cliff dive off Sunrise Rock
And I added one just for you . . .
27. Ditch a plan and follow your heart,
even if it scares you

I finish reading through the list aloud with Zayn next to me. Once I'm finished, I burst into tears again.

"Whoa, Autumn. It's okay," he says leaning in closer to me. He rubs my shoulder, which surprisingly doesn't repulse me. "You feelin' like you aren't ready to do these things?" he asks.

I shake my head. "Well, no, but it's not that . . . I just can't believe she's gone and I'm doing all this without her." Wiping away more tears, I take a sip from the cup of water he brought me. I add, "And to be quite honest, I am a chicken. I'm not a risk-taker."

Zayn pauses for a moment, licking his lips before biting them. He always used to do that when he was thinking. I used to think it was so hot. Okay, fine. It still freaking is. "It seems like a fairly low-risk list. No sky diving, no bungee jumping. I do get the toilet papering of Nick Hartzell's house though. That dude was a scumbag. But other than that, where are all the thrill-seeking adventures Summer was all about on this list?" He looks at me with eyebrows raised.

"Well, I told her we could make the list under the condition that it had be to things I agreed to."

He gives an understanding nod. "Well then, that's quite

the list there, but you've already done most of it by now, I'm guessing?" he asks.

"Hmm . . . honestly, no. That's what I'm saying. I'm still as much of a scaredy cat as I was the day we made this," I admit. "Half of these Summer had already done when we were younger, but she wanted me to do them with her. Like I can bury her in the sand all day, but I'd rather die than get buried in it."

"Scared no one will dig you back out, huh?"

"Um, yes. Exactly. I can't trust anyone," I say. As soon as the words leave my lips, I realize he probably thinks I'm directing that at him.

"Let's find you a pen so you can definitely cross out the ones you have done. Maybe it'll seem less intimidating then," he suggests.

I read through the list again. "Hmm, well number one is definitely done. Not that it's the dream job I thought it would be, but nevertheless, it was part of the list that I did."

"Teaching isn't what you expected it to be, huh?" he asks.

"Yeah, it's a long story. I'm considering a career change, but I've already been hit with so many dang changes that I might combust if I have to handle anymore," I answer honestly.

"I remember how much you hated change," he says. For some reason, I like that he remembers that about me. "So, what else have you already done then?"

"Thanks to yesterday's adventures, I now have taken a Four Horsemen shot and danced on a bar."

Zayn chokes on his own spit before laughing. "That makes so much more sense now! I was wondering why the hell you ordered that drink at Karma."

"Oof, you saw that?"

"Yeah, I heard Joe giving you a hard time about

ordering it. He seemed to be caught off guard about you doing it, too."

I nod. "Yeah, and for the record, I don't usually go around dancing on bars, either."

Zayn laughs. I look back to the list.

"You did fracture a part of your foot from the bar fall, so you've now broken a bone, right?" Zayn asks.

"Oh shit, you're right. Let's check that one off," I say.

He laughs briefly to himself before saying, "I was only thinking on my feet." He winks. "Get it?"

My eyes roll, but I allow a slight laugh to escape me. "Oh my god. Well, I guess you're entitled to make dad jokes now though," I offer. "Oh wait, and I'm crossing off 'flash or moon someone' as that was also accomplished last night."

"Um, what? No way! That doesn't count," Zayn says.

I take the pen to the paper and cross it off. "Excuse me, but you saw my whole butt. It counts," I say.

"Yeah, but it was on accident," he counters.

I think about it for a moment. "Ok, I'll put a half-check by it since it sort of counts. If I finish the list and still haven't, I'll plan to do it. Swear."

"Hah, you're starting to sound more like the Autumn I used to know," he says.

I pause for a moment, unsure if he means that in a good or bad way.

Zayn fills the silence. "Okay, Miss Parker, so which one of these do you want to do next?"

7

"Hey lady, how ya feeling?" Mason asks me as we walk out of the school building to the parking lot together.

"I'm doing a lot better now that my foot is back to normal. Head is still a little on the fritz with these terrible headaches," I admit.

He purses his lips. "Well, shit. I was going to see if you wanted to go grab some beers with me and Nat. I can tell she's feeling a bit left out since you and I work together now."

"Oh."

Waving a hand in front of me, he says, "It's all good, girl. Get some rest. We can raincheck."

I pause for a moment. "Well, it's honestly not my head that's the problem. I want to, but I actually have other plans tonight."

His eyebrows raise as he dramatically places his hand on his chest. "Oh, well excuse me, Miss Popular. What do you have planned?"

I grit my teeth. "Okay, I know what it sounds like, but it's not a date."

"So, it's not the head that's the problem. It's the heart. Let me guess . . . you're going out with a certain fireman, aren't you?" he teases.

I smirk. "Guilty."

"Well, well. Need I remind you this is the boy who crushed your heart into a million little pieces that took months to clean up? He sure never put out his own fire he started."

I can't help but chuckle. "Really, Mace?" I shrug. "But trust me, I haven't forgotten. We're just going for sushi so I can cross it off the WOLO list. Nothing more."

He gives a dragged out "okay" before adding, "Nat and I would've gotten sushi with you, but I know Mr. Mitchell heroically rescued you from your bar fall. And I know personally the man is harmless now that he has a kid. So, go on and enjoy your not-date date." He gives the last couple words emphasis with air quotes.

"Hah, well I promise you if I do like sushi, you, me, and Nat can go eat it as our next date."

He seems to like that answer because he blows me a kiss and gives me a wink. "That better happen, bitch. Love you! Go have fun." Mason is about to sit in his car when he taps the top of it briefly. "Oh, and please call or text if you need any fake emergencies to happen. We got your back, boo."

"Yeah, hopefully no more real emergencies. I'll keep you posted, love!" I blow him a kiss before we both get into our cars.

I sit in mine for a minute, clutching the steering wheel. Releasing a deep breath, I think, *Shit, is this a mistake? It's one meal with Zayn. That's it. And I probably won't even like sushi. Or him.*

"So, what do you suggest I try?" I ask Zayn as I look over the menu.

He snatches the menu from me and asks, "Do you trust me?"

I squint my eyes with uncertainty. *Is he for real right now?* It's feeling quite like the scene in *Aladdin* when he holds out his hand for Jasmine to get onto the magic carpet with him.

"Um yeah, don't answer that," Zayn says, letting out a laugh. "But seriously, trust me."

What would Summer do? I throw my hands in the air, surrendering the menu to him. "Fine, fine. What have I got to lose? I'm probably only going to eat a single grain of rice anyway."

He scoffs. "You better not. You have to at least try two whole pieces. Summer would never let you get away with a single grain tasting and you know it."

I take a deep breath. "You're one hundred percent right. I really need to suck it up and try it."

I watch as Zayn orders several different rolls for us. He orders with words like, "The SAT Roll, Caterpillar, Spider-man, Volcano, and Dynamite." I bust out in laughter when he asks for sides of "spicy mayo and eel sauce" for us to dip them in, too.

"That's quite the combination of sushi rolls I'm about to try. Feels like I'm sitting with a kid in my class making a fictional superhero salad or something," I tell him.

"Hah, I could see that. Riley would love making up fun ingredients for superhero supper," he says.

"Now that's an idea of our next writing assignment," I say. "How is Riley, by the way?"

"She's doing great. I spoke with her mom this morning, and she loved her first day, so kudos to you. You're doing a fantastic job already," I say encouragingly.

The server starts heading our way with . . . *a boat?*

"What is tha—oh my gosh, this is our meal?" I ask, shocked. "It's in a freakin'. . . boat! How cool is that!" I light up with excitement. I've never seen a sushi-filled boat before.

Zayn looks at the server. "First timers, am I right?"

She doesn't seem to play along with his sarcasm and asks if there's anything else she can get for us.

I search the table for a fork. "Uh, actually, could I get a fork?"

Zayn interjects, "Absolutely not. Please, do not bring her one. She needs to try sushi for the first time *the right way.*"

He looks at me apologetically. "Sorry, I didn't mean for that to come off as rude. But you for sure need to do this the most authentic way possible."

I consider this and pick up the chopsticks from the napkin. I look over at the way Zayn grasps them and I mimic him.

"Am I totally butchering this or what?"

"Believe it or not, no. You're doing great," he says before pointing to the roll with eel. "I think you'll like this one best so try it first. Pick it up just like I am." He demonstrates with his chopsticks. "Basically, you pick it up, dip it into the soy sauce, and then, shove the whole thing in your mouth. You'll want the fish on top to hit your tongue, so you get the full flavor."

"The whole thing in my mouth? It's huge," I say.

"That's what she said," he jokes.

I roll my eyes. "Ha ha, very funny." I pick it up with chopsticks and dip it into the soy sauce. "Okay, but for real. What if I don't like it?"

"I don't know, but what if you do?" he offers as rebuttal.

I decide to go for it and put the entire piece of sushi in my mouth. The whole thing. While using chopsticks.

"Nicely done, Miss Parker." He pauses for a moment, watching me as I chew. *It's delicious! How have I not been eating this my entire life?* I raise my eyebrow, trying to decide if I should admit to him how much I like it. I swallow and take a sip of my water.

"So, let's hear it. What's the official verdict?"

"I . . . well, I . . ." I say, scrunching up my nose playfully before busting out in laughter. "Oh to hell with joking, I loved it!"

"Ha, I knew you would," he says. "Which one do you want to try next?"

I don't even say another word. I pick up the next piece from another roll. *Dang, this one is equally delicious.*

After I swallow the second roll, I say, "You know what? I don't even care in the slightest what nasty things might be in these rolls, the combination of it all is delicious! Can we get more?"

Zayn laughs. "Okay, missy. Slow your roll—literally and figuratively."

"Don't tell me how to live my life," I tease.

He smirks, throwing up his hands in pretend protest. "Not sure what's spicier . . . you or these rolls."

He smiles at his own joke, and I can't help but love the way his dark eyes sparkle when he does.

"I'm just saying, sushi will fill you up much faster than you think, so let's finish these first."

"Okay, fine," I agree feeling like my heart is fuller than my stomach right now.

"Let's hear more about this WOLO list you and Summer made. When did you make it?" Zayn leans down on his elbow.

I clear my throat, remembering the exact reason why. Him. Well, to get over him.

"Uh, oh it's silly, really. She was trying to cheer me up after our breakup. We stayed up almost all night laughing and planning these crazy or as she believed not-so-crazy things that we'd do together as a bucket list."

"Ah, at least I inspired something good after all." He inches forward. "It sounds great. So what's on the list that you're most afraid to do?" he asks.

I've thought about this a lot, but for some reason I can't really pinpoint it right now. "Hmm, it's tough to say. Cliff diving and the blind date are the most intimidating for sure, but I think the one I fear the most is the tattoo."

His left eyebrow raises. "The tattoo?"

I nod. "Yeah, I think it feels so permanent, and I don't want to get something stupid that I'll regret later. As you're probably aware, I try to live with no regrets."

"Makes sense. Any clue what you would get?" he asks.

"I think I have something in mind, but I wouldn't know until I'm actually sitting in the chair."

"Makes sense," he says.

"Yeah," I say. "What about you? Have any tats?"

"I do actually. This one here"— he rolls up his sleeve— "of a light saber fight between Luke Skywalker and Darth Vader. I also have one on my chest and one on my upper back. Upper back is angel wings with my birthday—the day my mom passed—and the other is a penguin, which my dad told me was my mom's favorite animal. So they're all symbolic of my mom. Well, except my *Star Wars* one."

"Sounds pretty cool," I admit. "I love that, Zayn. I'm sure your mom would be so proud of you, Mr. Firefighter *and* dad now. I can't believe it."

"I like to think so, too. And thanks," he says.

"Anyway, I like tattoos that do have meaning, but I guess if I loved something as much as you love *Star Wars*, that'd work, too."

"For sure," he says before taking a sip of his water. "Does Liam have tattoos?"

I'm jarred by his question. "Um, yes. He did, err—does. Only one across his back. An eagle. He never really shared its significance, but I think he just likes it."

"Oh, okay. Sorry I asked. Was just curious," he admits. "Without sounding too nosy, can I ask what happened . . . between you and Liam? If you don't want to answer, I understand."

I hesitate for a moment. "I—uh, no it's fine. I think I'm ready to talk about it. But, well, one day he just left me. Filed for divorce without much conversation."

"What? That asshole! Why? How could he?"

I pause and notice as he briefly closes his eyes, probably realizing he did that exact thing to me a decade ago.

"Err, sorry about that. I know how that sounded now, but in all seriousness, I can't wrap my head around why he would do that."

I fidget with my chopsticks, mulling over how much I want to share with him.

"You know what?" Zayn raises his hands. "It's not my business, and I do apologize for asking. You absolutely don't have to share."

I consider if there's any risk in actually opening up to Zayn about Liam.

"No, it's okay," I say. "You know, to be honest, I'm not sure myself what happened. One minute, things seemed perfect, and the next they weren't. Part of it doesn't feel real. Seems like a distant dream."

He nods before taking another bite.

I continue, "It's normal for people to ask. I really don't know if he met someone else, cheated on me, or if we were maxing out our time with fake happiness. Either way, he wasn't supportive with Summer. That's when I knew we were truly over. And as you know, I regret not being here for her final days. Sure, I take full blame and responsibility, but my actions were influenced by him . . . unfortunately."

His eyes widen at my admission.

"Wow, well thanks for sharing that with me, Autumn. I'm sorry for all that—Summer getting sick and for Liam being a dick. You really deserve so much better."

I fight back the tears, taking a long sip of water. I clear my throat. "Thanks."

We both glance down and continue eating until the boat of sushi is empty.

I break the silence. "Oh my, that was so delicious! I'm so relieved it wasn't terrible like I was expecting," I admit.

"I'm relieved, too," Zayn says.

"Thank you for this. It means a lot that you took the time to help me check an item off the WOLO list."

"I'm happy to do so," he says. "I hope you don't mind, but I have something else big planned for us this evening, too." He clears his throat. "To help you check off another item from the list. You up for it?"

I stare at him for a moment. Before I can reply, the server comes over with the check. He quickly snatches it, leaving me with zero chance of snagging it first.

"You don't have to buy me sushi," I say.

"I know I don't have to do anything. But I want to." He smiles another glowing grin and I can't help but feel a slight flush in my cheeks.

"Well anyway, I haven't really had time to plan out exactly what I'm doing from the list and when," I tell him. I really do want to plan for it.

He looks away for a moment. "Okay, no worries. Just thought I'd throw it out there, but I understand."

I take one final bite of sushi. "Thank you, Zayn," I say.

"You're welcome," he says.

A moment of courage hits me. Hopefully I don't regret this. "You know what? Screw it. Where we headed next?"

WE PULL into the parking lot of a paint-and-sip place. I look over to Zayn, raising an eyebrow. "A painting place? Does this count as learning something new?"

He shrugs. "Wait, do you paint professionally, and I don't know it?"

I let out a laugh. "No, I've actually never painted anything unless you count high school art class. Well, okay, I've painted with some watercolors with the kids before, but that's about it."

"Good to know. I'd say it fits the WOLO list perfectly, then. Wait, have you ever painted an axolotl before?"

"You're joking." My arms fold across my chest. *He can't be serious.* "We aren't really painting an axolotl, are we?"

He unbuckles his seatbelt and flashes me a smile. "Yeah, I think it's riding a narwhal or something."

He really is unbelievable. I watch him walk around to greet me on the passenger side. Even though he can't see me, I roll my eyes.

He opens the door for me. "Come on, granny. Let's get in before we're late."

The woman at the front of the store greets us. Her messy bun and paint-splattered apron instantly give away she's the artist. "Welcome! Have you guys been here before?" she asks.

We both shake our heads. I find relief knowing he also hasn't done one of these classes before.

"Well then, consider this the perfect date night for you two," the artist offers with a smile. "Come. Follow me."

Zayn and I exchange quick awkward glances while the woman leads us to our seats with the canvases already set on the table. All paint materials are readily available to the side of them, too.

"This is so cute," I admit.

"It is, actually."

I get close to my chair and say, "By the way, this is *not* a date."

"I know. Don't worry."

Relief washes over me. It is starting to feel like a date, but I need to relax. He's helping me knock off some items on the WOLO list. That's it. Nothing more.

We both notice the bar simultaneously. "Would you like some wine?" he asks.

I hesitate for a moment, glancing around the room full of paintings before nodding. "Wait, do you think I'm in the clear now to drink? The doctor said to give it a week, but I don't know if I should wait longer."

"Let's just not get wasted, but I think if you have just a glass, it'll be fine. No pressure though," he says. "Truly, no obligation. We don't have to have alcohol to have a good time."

"Very true. And I appreciate the no pressure thing. Believe it or not, being around big city life and snobby people, I've built up some tough skin to be able to say no. Well, you already know I've never been a big partier. Liam on the other hand," I say, stopping myself before saying more about him. He's already ruined so much for me. I don't need him continuing to ruin things by bringing him up.

"Yeah, no I get that. When you're around people who do nothing but alter their state of mind, it gets easier to turn them down though," he offers.

I'm a bit startled by his statement, but it comforts me. I tuck my hair behind my ear. "You know what, I'd love just a glass of dry red."

"Exactly what I was thinking," he says. "Go ahead and have a seat. I'll grab it."

While Zayn is over at the bar, I decide to use the restroom.

When I make it to the bathroom, I stare at myself in the mirror for a moment.

"Autumn, this isn't a date," I say out loud to myself. "Stop being so nervous."

Another woman walks in, and I'm hoping she didn't hear me giving myself a pep talk. She flashes me a polite smile and heads into a nearby stall. Turning on the faucet, I splash some water on my face, wash my hands, and leave quietly.

I spot Zayn glancing down at his phone near our section.

"You bored already, Mr. Mitchell?" I tease. "We just got here."

He looks up at me and his jaw drops slightly. "Oh, there you—"

"Wait," I say, pausing to look around and back down at his phone. "Did you think I ditched you?"

His lips move to the side of his mouth, and he raises his hands. "Guilty."

"Don't be silly. You, uh, well . . . you've been a huge help already with the list and I'm glad we're here."

We're interrupted by one of the artists.

"Okay, ladies and gentlemen. Hopefully by now, you've gotten your drinks and found yourself a seat. For those of you who've been here before, welcome back. And for those who are new to us this evening, welcome. And no worries. We are our own worst critics, and I'll be sure to go through everything step-by-step. But remember, just have fun." She does a quick check of everyone in the room, flashing a heartwarming smile. "As you know, tonight is quite a fun one. Everyone, meet Allie the Axolotl."

I bite my lip, feeling extremely nervous to paint an axolotl for the first time.

"Told ya," he whispers.

"Where's the narwhal?" I chime back.

Zayn chuckles. "Okay, maybe I fabricated that part a bit."

"You know," I smile. "For someone who is supposed to be earning my trust back, you have a funny way of showing it."

He holds his to his heart again, imitating a fake wound. "Oof. You got me there, Miss Parker."

The artist shoots us a glare, and we both go silent and serious again.

"Anyway, a fun fact is that axolotls can be viewed as great healers. They symbolize good health and potential for healing and renewal of oneself. They are fascinating creatures that can change themselves quite significantly, whether it's their color, features, or size. So, remember that if you do make any mistakes, it's really just the axolotl going through another life transformation."

I stare intently, soaking in the information. Who had a clue that axolotls were this cool?

Zayn leans in next to me to whisper, "I didn't realize this was gonna get so deep."

Instead of laughing, I nod, continuing to absorb the artist's words and learning about the powers of the axolotl.

8
☑ Get a Unique Pet

I think I'm finally starting to feel like myself again. Being back in Lake View isn't so terrible. Aside from the loneliness, I'm getting into a much better routine. Mom has been staying at the beach house for the past couple nights with me while Zayn has been working at the fire station. We've been texting, and I won't lie, I look forward to receiving messages from him. I briefly shudder at my admission.

The door cracks open and I see Mom's head peek through. When she sees I'm awake, she enters with a tray in her hand. "Good morning, sweetie. I made some coffee and your favorite cinnamon rolls for breakfast."

"Mmmm, I thought that's what I was smelling." I sit up in the bed. Mom makes her way over and takes a seat on the edge of it. "Thanks, Mom," I tell her. "For everything."

"You're more than welcome. I've rather enjoyed getting to take care of one of my babies again, just like old times." I notice her voice crack a bit at the word 'babies.' I think as she said it, she reminded herself there's only one of us now. I miss Summer so much.

"Yeah, I've enjoyed being taken care of," I admit with a smile.

"So, how you holding up? You seem to be a busy bee lately. You're not overdoing it, right? I mean, my goodness, sweetheart, you were just in the hospital not long ago."

I yawn while doing a big stretch. I didn't realize she'd

want to have a full-on chat this early on a Saturday morning, but it's fine.

"Hmm . . . I have to admit, it's all going well. I think this school year is promising. I know I always freak out about big changes, but this time feels good. It feels better being back here than I ever could have anticipated."

"I'm so happy to hear that, honey. Glad you're giving teaching another go, but remember, your generation has multiple careers throughout their lifetime now. It's okay to not stick with something that you don't love, or even like, for that matter." Mom pauses and gives a smile. "I know how much you love those kids, though. But hopefully you'll have some of your own one day and then those will be the ones that you'll prioritize above everything else." Mom leans in closer to me and cups my chin. "And it's all worth it."

I give her a genuine smile. "I know, I think it simply feels so stressful that all this stuff is happening to me at once. I'm back home, teaching in my old elementary school, no longer with Liam, and Zayn is in my life way more than I wanted or planned." I shrug.

"Autumn, I know you've been through so much, but you've been a little closed off lately. More than usual. I hope it's alright for me to ask, but what ended up happening between you and Liam?"

Tears form in the corners of my eyes. "You know Mom, I'm not even sure. We had terrible communication. Nothing like you and dad. He never opened up to me about his feelings and he always pushed mine to the side like they were meaningless. In fact, I didn't even know he wanted a divorce. I found out on accident."

SIX MONTHS AGO

My gaze turns to the door of the coffee shop exactly as Liam walks in wearing his usual Armani suit and tie, his blonde hair gelled back. Smiling, he heads towards me. I notice some young girls at a table nearby acting giddy over his presence. Don't get me wrong, he's an attractive guy. Hell, I did marry him after all. But the past few years all we've done is go through the motions. Summer calls him my roommate, but even him being a roommate would be an upgrade considering how infrequent he's home. Liam pulls out his chair, resting his suit jacket on the back of it.

"Hey there, my beautiful wife." I cringe, knowing he's probably trying to impress the people around us more than he's actually giving me a compliment.

He takes a seat at the table, and the server comes over. "What can I get for you, sir?"

"A venti black coffee, please," he replies.

I can't help but roll my eyes. "So, you know the lingo here, huh?" I try easing the tension that fills the room, making it harder to breathe with every inhale.

He shrugs. "Yeah, they're just like Starbucks." Liam pauses before adding, "I've been here a few times with clients."

Of course he has. When has he ever not been to a place before with clients? The barista set our coffees down, and politely whispers, "Let me know if there's anything else you need."

"Thank you," I say before taking a sip of my cappuccino.

Liam looks at me and asks, "So, why are you off today?" The fact that he doesn't have a clue about my schedule confirms my decision even more.

"Um, school got out this past Friday for spring break. Remember I had the spring festival that I spent weeks planning for the kids?" Surprise hit his face for a moment before he nods, acting as though he actually remembers. "Well, anyway, I'm glad you were able to meet me here. We both know I hate change, so

please know that I'm seriously considering this. I need you not to take it lightly because I really feel like this is what I need to do, so I'd like to add it to our plan for the year. Anyway, I'm blabbering on and on . . . but I'm wondering how you feel about us possibly moving to my hometown? Even if just temporarily."

The surprise in his face turns to full-blown shock. "I'm sorry —wh—what? Move? To Lake View? Come on, Autumn, you can't be serious. You said it yourself that you'd never move back there even if someone paid you a billion dollars to do so."

"Yes, I'm serious about Lake View, or even just somewhere close to it. Liam, I really feel like I need to be closer to my family in North Carolina right now. Trust me, I can't believe I'm saying it either."

He scoffs. "This is a terrible idea. I have to put my foot down with this. It's a no."

"Put your foot down? Excuse me! You're not even going to hear me out first?" The desperation in my voice announces itself.

He blows out a large breath. "It's not that, honey. It's just that I know what's best for us and moving to your hometown is not a part our plan. You know this. Plus, my business is booming. Aren't you happy with all these things I've provided for you?"

I take a moment to process his response. We've always been a good team because we're so alike—we love to be prepared and plan all we can. Maybe we can't plan our whole lives as well as we thought we could. After a moment, I say, "I am so appreciative of your hard work and all the things we have, but I really need to be with my family right now."

This isn't just me wanting to move back to be closer to family. I have to do it for Summer. I lean forward in an attempt to straighten my posture. I need to be with Summer, so I need to act like Summer. She would never beat around the bush with the important stuff, so I'm just going to jump straight to it. I should be the one putting my foot down, damn it.

Liam beats me to it. "Look, I will fly you out to your family whenever you need. We can afford it, but I don't think we should just uproot our wonderful lives here in Connecticut and move to that tiny beach town. I can't believe how completely selfish you're being right now."

Ouch. He knows that the last thing I ever want to be described as is selfish. My eyes briefly shift toward the Rolex watch peeking out from under his button-down Armani shirt.

"Excuse me," I scoff. "Are you not even curious as to why I need to move back? You claim I'm being selfish, and yet you won't even bother to hear me out. It's an instant no for you at the mere mention of it."

He uses his hands to push himself away from the table. His defense mode activates. "You really invited me to coffee to pick a fight with me today, didn't you?" He crosses his arms, but then lifts his right one up to hold up his head. He adds, "Autumn, I can't do this anymore."

Those words trigger me. They bring me back to the night Zayn left me. But with Zayn, I never saw it coming. I was naive and thought we'd last forever. Our relationship wasn't conventionally perfect, but it was perfect for me.

Sometimes I wonder if that's why I said yes to Liam's proposal in the first place. I didn't want that unpredictable love, with passion so hot that it sets your soul aflame. Everyone knows that kind only burns out quickly. I wanted the opposite—steady and predictable—just like what my parents have. And at the time, Liam checked all my boxes: (1) comes from good family, (2) holds a stable job, (3) is financially savvy, (4) likes to plan and set future goals, and (5) wants exactly two kids. Most importantly, I liked that we both shared an aversion to risk and a need for control—we tried to plan out everything. He was supposed to be the perfect partner who would never hurt me. Liam and I make sense. We're predictable. Unfortunately, the only thing unpredictable about my love with Liam is that it's been a complete facade. All we do is pretend to be something we're not.

"Liam," I reach for his hand, but he moves it away before I can grab it. I withdraw my hand, briefly feeling the physical rejection trying to overpower the emotional. Closing my eyes, I take a deep breath before I exhale and release those excruciatingly painful words. "Summer is dying."

A tear forms in his left eye as it stares so deeply into my own. His lips part and his jawslowly drops. He doesn't say anything, and neither do I. What is there really to say after that bomb has been dropped? I watch as his forehead falls into both of his hands. He rubs his temples with his palms until they meet his cheeks. He glances around the coffee shop until looking back to me. He releases his hands from his face.

"Autumn, I—" He pauses. "I—I don't really even know what to say. Shit. I'm so sorry." I know he is sorry. This is the genuine Liam I fell in love with. Deep down, he really is a good guy. But he's become so consumed with himself, infatuated by the superficial life we've both been living. Surprise finds me when I see his hand reaching out for mine. He cups my hand in his, and I don't pull back. After all these years, he's still a safe space for me. I exhale. I know he cares about me and my family, and I know he loves me.

"Thank you. I'm sorry, too. If I knew what to say, you know I'd say it," I say. He nods his head in agreement. We both know how talkative I always am.

He releases my hand. Bringing his fist to his mouth, he blows his breath into it. He looks back to me. "So, how long does she have? Her cancer returned?"

I close my eyes to try to protect my heart from those words: Cancer. Returned.

Breast cancer. Yet again. Why is life so damn cruel sometimes? I can't imagine life without my sister. She is more a part of me than I am part of myself. Summer knows me inside and out, and better than anyone ever can or will.

We allow each other to just be for a while. Sitting, merely

existing together in silence, in the middle of a noisy coffee shop. The barista interrupts the silence when he asks if there's anything else he can get for us. I manage to shake my head, but my eyes don't stray from Liam's.

A few moments later, the check arrives. We both return to pretending everything is normal. Liam signs the check, thanks the server a final time, and gives me the ready-to-leave nod.

As he stands up and grabs his jacket from behind the chair, his work bag falls to the ground. He instantly picks up his laptop to inspect its condition. I bend down, trying to help organize all the papers that fell out by placing them back into folders for him. I grab one that looks like a legal document. It's labeled, 'Petition for Dissolution of Marriage.' My whole body tenses. I look over to him, but he is still ensuring there's nothing wrong with his laptop. I let out a long breath, shakily placing the final papers back into the sleeve of a folder. I grab the couple of pens that fell out, too, before standing up.

"Here you go," I say, handing him the spilled contents from the bag. I'm not sure if I should bring it up. What if it's not even his? Or what if it is? I mean, sure, we've been going through the motions the past couple years, but neither of us has ever mentioned the word 'divorce.'

Once he places the re-packed satchel onto his shoulder, he reaches his hand out for mine. I allow my hand to fall into his, to help steady my weak knees more than anything.

"So, where do we go from here?" Liam asks as if it's just an ordinary day for us. There's so much to unpack from this loaded question, but I allow my shoulders to answer him with a shrug.

"Here, how about we chat outside for a bit before I head back to the office?" His arm spreads itself around my lower back, still protecting me as if I'm his. As if he isn't hiding divorce papers in his bag. My stomach grumbles with fear of so many unknowns. He's probably about to bring it up the minute we make our way out that door.

He holds the door to the coffee shop open for me as I step outside. Outside of the door. Outside of my comfort zone. Outside of my reality. Outside of my perfect life.

"Oh wow, what an asshole," Mom says.

We both laugh. Mom never cusses. She clears her throat. "Well, I'm sorry he did that to you. He wasn't for you, and I had a gut feeling about that from the beginning."

"I know. Everyone did but me, I guess. He seemed so perfect at the time though. When we first started, it felt so much like what you and Dad have," I say as my shoulders shrug. "I don't think I'm meant to have a relationship like yours though."

She grabs my chin. "Oh honey, you will find love again. I just know it. And it's easy to say it's great from the outside looking in, but your father and I put in a lot of hard work to have what we have. I have no doubt that you'll find someone who's worth the work." She releases my chin and gives me a wink.

A tear falls down my cheek and I nod. Mom leans in closer and wraps her arms around me.

"Thanks, Mom. I hope so."

"Well, even with him being a big old jerk and you winding up back in Lake View, I'm so happy you're home." She gives me a final big squeeze before releasing me. "What do you say we hit up some stores today and do a little shopping—just you and me?"

"Love you, mom," I say and smile. "Alright, let's do it."

She heads toward the door and looks back. "I'm going to start getting ready then. Eat your breakfast, and we'll aim to leave in about an hour. How's that sound?"

I nod my head while taking a large bite into the cinnamon roll.

AN HOUR LATER, I meet Mom in the kitchen. I load my plate and mug into the dishwasher.

"So, where would you like to go to today?" mom asks me.

"Hmmm . . . well, I know you probably weren't expecting this, but I'm thinking the pet store," I say, flashing a big smile across my face. I debate telling her about completing the WOLO list now, but I still want to keep it to myself.

Her eyebrow raises. "Oh, really?"

"Yeah, that way I won't be totally alone like you and Dad got me all freaked out about," I say.

I watch as my mom clasps her hands together in excitement. "Oh yay! Let's go pick out a dog from the pet store today, then."

"Well, I'm not set on a dog, but I'd love for you to help me pick out a new furry friend."

"Alright, sounds like a plan to me," she says.

"Perfect. Let's go then. I'll drive," I say, picking the keys up off the counter and tossing them into my crossbody bag.

We get in the car and head to the local pet store. Mom doesn't say too much to me on the way, but I can tell she's been holding back tears. She mentions missing Summer. When I tell her I do too, I feel that familiar stinging in my eyes.

When we finally pull into a parking spot at the pet store, my mom doesn't move to open the door once I've turned the engine off. I sense a shift in her entire mood.

"Hey sweetie, I want you to be honest with me. You and

Summer were thick as thieves. Losing her has been hard for all of us, but you seem to be actively trying to avoid your feelings when I mention her."

I let out a small sigh and look into my mother's eyes. They look just like Summer's—a gorgeous, crystal blue. It's silly to admit, but while I did get my green eyes from Dad, I was always a little jealous that Summer got Mom's eyes. I grew up wanting to be exactly like Summer. And now, in what feels like a blink of an eye, she's gone. Who will I look up to now?

"I'm okay." I have to be the strong one for her and Dad. I've always been the responsible, have-your-shit-together one of us. Summer was basically a wildflower, and I—well, I was a low-maintenance homebody orchid. Granted, I need more than a couple of ice cubes a week to stay alive, but for the most part, I've preferred to play it safe in life.

"I know you will be, but that doesn't mean you have to force yourself to be so strong right now. It's okay to feel the way you do. You don't need to pressure yourself with making sure others' emotions are in good hands if it means you're sacrificing your own."

More tears begin to well up in my eyes. How is it possible to cry this much? I'd spent the last few months hopping on planes back and forth from Connecticut to here when we found out Summer's breast cancer had returned and reached stage four. We've cried so much together knowing the inevitable was coming. But I missed her final day, which I think is what has broken me the most. I should've been here. I should've moved here and not let Liam stop me. I never trust myself when I should be trusting my own intuition more than anyone else. And now, I'd do anything just to go back to a simpler time with Summer.

My mom reaches into the glovebox. She pulls out a

small pack of tissues. She never misses a beat when it comes to knowing what people need at the exact moment they need it. As soon as I'm done wiping tears and supposed-waterproof mascara off my face, she leans in with a bear hug. Squeezing me tight enough that my arms close into my chest, I'm secretly wishing she'll never let go.

She turns back to me and whispers, "Autumn, it'll be okay. I promise."

I want to trust my mom and believe it really is okay. That everything will be fine. People always say, 'this too shall pass.' But what if it doesn't? What if that's simply not true? Summer was my person. More than Liam ever was, even though I convinced myself that he was.

"Thanks, Mom. I do think I've been so overwhelmed by everything that it's making me feel numb. Being in the hospital the first week I got here didn't help," I tell her and manage to smile again.

She releases a chuckle before saying, "Well, that is true. You've been through a lot in just a short amount of time. Now, let's go find you the perfect pet."

When we enter the pet store, my mom heads straight for the dogs. As much as I love dogs and always begged Liam for one, I feel like I need something more low main-tenance. I point towards the small animals and fish and tell Mom that I'm going to check them out first. Standing near the case of rabbits, I hear, "Hi Ms. Parker! Are you getting a pet?" I look up to see Riley Mitchell, Zayn's daughter. But she's not with Zayn. She's with Samantha Leeman.

"Yes," I look back to Riley. "I'm looking for a little buddy to keep me company now that I've moved back here. What are you guys up to?" I ask nonchalantly, hoping to find out why the two of them are together right now.

Samantha hears us chatting and her eyes light up when she sees me. "Autumn, how exciting to see you here today.

We're getting Riley her first pet today!" I take note of her use of the word, 'we.' My heart starts beating rapidly and my stomach churns in knots.

I look back to Riley, trying to stay focused. "Oh, that's awesome, Riley. Do you know what you're going to get?"

"I want a bunny," she says.

"Good choice. They're so cute," I say. I look back and forth between the two of them, trying to determine if Sam is Riley's mom when my own mom taps me on the shoulder.

"Honey, you've got to come see this puppy," she insists.

I tell Riley and Sam good luck with picking out the perfect bunny as my hand gives an awkward wave.

We end up leaving the store roughly half an hour later with not just a perfect pet, but one that's perfect for me in particular—a hedgehog. Mom rolled her eyes when I first picked him up and announced he was the only one for me.

We make our way back to the car and mom helps me load the hedgehog's cage into the back. She waves her index finger up and down and says, "Now, you be a good boy and enjoy your first car ride."

I smile. I can tell he's already growing on her.

When I finally get into the driver's seat, I sit there for a moment to process seeing Riley with Sam in the store. It doesn't make any sense as to why Zayn and Sam would have a kid together. I try to compute the math quickly, realizing that Riley is only a year younger than when Zayn and I were together. Did Zayn stay here to be with Sam?

Mom doesn't add anymore on the subject, but simply asks, "I can't believe you have a hedgehog now. Have you thought of a name for this little guy yet?"

"Hmmm," I think aloud for a moment. I could name him Liam as a joke, but then I'll have to continue saying Liam's name much longer than I'd prefer. I look towards the backseat at the little guy in the cage. He's curled up into a ball, guarding off any potential danger and showing off only his quills.

"Yes, I've got it. Quinton. Mom, meet Quinton the Hedgehog."

9

I feel like I'm back in high school on our first date with the way my nerves feel right now. I look over at Zayn and catch him looking at me. I flash him a quick, nervous smile before I ask, "Alright, mister. Where are you taking me?"

Zayn shakes his head and releases a small chuckle. "I thought we'd agreed that it'd be a surprise."

"True, but this drive is so long, and it feels like we're headed to the middle of nowhere." I stare out the window of the truck. "Look at this sunset view!"

"Absolutely gorgeous," he says.

I glance over to Zayn to see if he's actually agreeing with me, but I catch him only looking at me.

My eyebrow arches. "So, you're really not going to tell me?" I ask.

He caves. "Fine, do you really want to know?"

I shake my head. "Of course, I do . . . we both know I

hate surprises. I need a plan so I can mentally prepare. It was bad enough trusting a guy on how I should dress for the evening."

Nodding, he says, "Okay, well . . . I'm not sure if it's your thing anymore since I know you've been living in a rich city, but it's a country bar, about fifteen more miles out."

"Oh, hmm. You're driving us somewhere far, in the middle of nowhere, that I've never been before," I pause and turn my head completely toward him. "Zayn Mitchell, are you planning to murder me out here?"

He laughs. "If that is in fact the plan, you really think I'm about to tell that to you willy-nilly?"

"Fair enough," I say. "So, do you have Pandora or Spotify?"

He shakes his head. "Call me old school, but this truck still has a CD player and basic radio."

"Seriously? Why even bother having an iPhone then?" I ask him.

"I mean, I'm not completely living under a rock," he chuckles. "I just think what I have is totally fine."

"Hmm okay. Where are your CDs?"

His hand lowers on the steering wheel and he glances my way. "I just cleaned out the truck for tonight, so I took them out and forget to put them back in."

"Alrighty then," I say. "Radio it is!" I lean forward and turn on the radio, determined to find a country music station. When I hear Jason Aldean's voice coming through, I stop. "Got to set the right vibe for the bar."

Zayn nods, flashing me a big, cheesy grin. A few moments later, and we're both singing at the top of our lungs to Luke Bryan on the radio. Feels just like old times again.

He makes a final right turn, heading onto a dirt road. I

decide to lower the volume to ask if we've made it.

As soon as he turns a final corner, I see the jam-packed bar. He nods and answers, "Yup. Here we are."

The neon sign, reading 'Daisy's Roadhouse' flashes above us. "If I had known we'd really be going to a country bar, I'd have worn my boots." I hop out the truck and walk around to him.

"You own a pair of cowboy boots?" he asks.

I laugh and shake my head. "Fine, you caught me. I don't, but I would've bought some."

We walk up to the bar and the back of his hand brushes mine for a moment. Instant chills prickle down the back of my neck. Zayn flashes me a genuine smile, and I swear I'm going to melt into a puddle right here.

"After you," he says while jokingly bowing down for me to enter.

Zayn follows behind me as we enter. I look around for a little before staring at him with wide eyes. "Um, what is *that*?" I ask, pointing past the bar over to a giant mechanical bull.

He releases a chuckle and says, "*That* there is the whole purpose we're here."

"Shit," I say before blowing out a breath.

Zayn lifts his hands as if he's getting pulled over by the cops. "Hey hey, no turning back now. It's on the list. Unless your foot still isn't better. I know it's been a while, but I want to make sure."

Without thinking, I grab his hand and lead us over to the bar. "I'm definitely going to need a drink first."

"Another Four Horsemen?" he asks.

My eyes widen as I cover my hand with my mouth, pretending to feel sick. "Absolutely not. Been there, done that."

Zayn stands by the bar with no attention from the

bartender. I scoot next to him, and he's suddenly paid attention to. *Men.*

He tosses up his hands to signal, 'What the hell?' I roll my eyes. "Right? It's ridiculous it's still like this," I say.

The bartender stands there waiting for me to order, so I get an IPA for Zayn and the usual vodka soda with lime for me. The bartender grunts before turning around to grab our drinks.

Zayn pulls out his wallet, tossing his card on the bar top, indicating with a thumbs up to the ignorant bartender that he is cool with starting a tab.

The drinks appear in front of us, and we clink them together. I'm about to say cheers when I instead, opt for, "YOLO?!"

He responds with, "Nah, WOLO," and we both slowly take a sip.

I pause, enjoying the fact that I'm once again able to let loose. I set my drink down and ask, "So how are things at the fire station lately? Rescue any more cats this week?" I tease.

He laughs. "Ha ha, I won't lie, things are pretty quiet on the fire side in this small town. I'm much more of a pet-rescuer, it feels."

"Wow, I was only joking. I guess it's kind of nice that you don't have to put out fires every second of the day, though, right?"

He nods, taking a sip of his IPA. "Yeah, it is nice. But I want to help more. I went into this job expecting to do more than rescue cats."

"I understand that. I went into teaching expecting to do more than herding cats."

Zayn spits out a bit of his beer from laughing and grabs a napkin off the counter to wipe his mouth. "You know, you're a lot funnier than I remember, Miss Parker."

Not sure if it's him or the drink, but warmth makes its way from my cheeks down my entire body. I also want to be annoyed at him calling Miss Parker so much, but for some reason, I like how he says it. *Stop it. Don't fall for this heartbreaker twice,* I remind myself.

"In all seriousness though, how is the school year down here treating you?"

I shrug, noticing the music getting louder. "I—well, I'm shocked, to be honest. I was starting to dread teaching, but maybe I just needed a change of scenery."

He nods. "That's good to hear."

"Yeah, so far, I'm glad I gave it a second chance," I admit —to both him and myself.

"So, you're a believer in second chances, eh?"

"Um—" I clear my throat. "I guess so. Sometimes." My cheeks flush harder. *I really walked myself right into that one, didn't I?*

Luckily for me, he just continues the conversation. "Well, I know Riley bug is so happy you're her teacher. She's doing so well this year, thanks to you," he says.

"Oh, stop it." I wave a hand at him. "Riley is a smart, super sweet girl. She's a great kid, Zayn."

"Thanks, that means a lot. I try," he says. "Here comes the bartender. Ready for another?"

"Yes, please. But I think this one will be my last for the night. Don't need to be puking when I get on the bull. That is *IF* I get on the bull, I clarify.

He squints his eyes. "Don't back out now."

I grit my teeth as the bartender drops off our new drinks. I pick mine up, move the straw to the side and chug it back. I decide that even if I don't get on the bull tonight, I still need an answer to a question that's been on my mind since the pet shop. "So, I've been meaning to ask, is Riley's mom Samantha Leeman?"

He opens his mouth to answer, but then the music stops for a moment and a loud voice calls over the mic, "Who dares to go next? Anyone else ready to tackle Billy the Bull?"

I look at Billy himself, trying to gauge whether or not I'm ready to go through with this. I tip back my drink once more to ensure I've gotten every last drop before slamming it down to announce, "Yup. I'm doing it. Summer would've never let me back out of this."

I take a deep breath. "You're gonna watch me, right?"

"I wouldn't miss it for the world," he says with a smile.

I head over to the middle-aged man with the microphone who gives a snarky laugh at my presence.

"I'd like a ride, please" I say with confidence.

"You got this, Autumn!" Zayn shouts, walking closer to the bull-riding area. It's basically a giant circle with padding and a fake bull in the middle.

The man whose long, gray braid hangs down over a Harley Davidson shirt under a leather jacket asks, "You sure about that, sweetheart?"

I cringe but answer, "I'm sure."

"Okay. Name?"

"Autumn Parker."

He stares at me with arched eyebrows for a moment. "Okay, Parker. Fill out this form and you'll be all set." He hands me a paper on a clipboard.

When I get to the bottom to sign my name, the man says, "Alright, you'll want to hop on by using the foot grip where the saddle is. One hand should grab onto the center bar while the other is in the air. Hold onto that center bar as long as you can and try to use your body weight to balance out the bucks. If you can hold on for longer than ten seconds, I'll speed it up. Any questions?"

At this point I'm so shocked I'm going through with this, so I shake my head in response.

I walk into the padded area and pause for a moment to toss my hair up into a ponytail. I whisper, "This is for you, Summer," as I slowly mount the mechanical bull. Fear rages through my body. I steady my shaky hand by gripping tightly onto the center bar.

The man waits over by the machine and I flash him a signal to start up the bull. I raise my left hand in the air as the guy announces into the mic, "Hey folks, let's see how long Miss Autumn Parker is able to hold her own on Billy. Here we go, in three . . . two . . . one . . . YEEHAW!" The audience yells out a resounding, "YEEHAW!"

The bull starts to buck back and forth. I try to stay determined, but I can't help but scream a little bit with each buck. The mechanical bull spins around quickly, and in the blink of an eye, it tosses me into the air. Within seconds, my back meets the padded floor. I yell breathlessly as I lie there feeling like the wind was knocked out of me. Pain throbs throughout my backside, and I consider if I've now broken something else.

Owww. The man stops the bull and comes over to me, offering his hand. I breathe in through my nostrils and grab hold of it to help me stand to my feet. I place my hand on my lower back and look up to see Zayn outside of the ring.

"Autumn? You okay? You doin' alright?" he shouts out.

I give him a thumbs up. Zayn smiles and shows me a double thumbs up in return.

"You made it six seconds, Parker," the man says.

"Thanks. That's five more than I thought," I admit.

Once I'm out of the designated bull-riding area, Zayn meets me. He instantly replaces my hand on my back with his, and I don't mind it.

"Whoa there, missy! You did it. How you feeling?" he asks.

"My damn back is killing me," I say. "But I did it, Zayn! I can't believe it. Summer would be proud. And probably laughing her ass off, too."

He flashes me a smile before motioning to the bartender for some water. "Actually, do you want another vodka soda?"

"Eh, if Four Horsemen shot didn't make me invincible while dancing on a bar the other night, I'm pretty sure there's little hope for me, now. Water sounds great."

The bartender drops off some water. As I take a sip, Zayn asks, "You want to call it a night?"

I contemplate it for a moment. I really am having such a good time, and I'm not really ready to leave. "Nah, not yet. Maybe one more drink?"

He shakes his head and laughs. "Okay, Miss Parker. If you insist."

"Sweet Home Alabama" starts playing as the bartender makes us another round of drinks. As soon as we get them, I take a few sips of mine and then decide to be bold. "Wanna dance?"

"Is your back well enough to do so?"

"Won't know unless I try, right?"

"Well then, in that case, I thought you'd never ask," he says, leading me out onto the dance floor. We dance playfully, both singing loudly to the music.

When the song ends, we head back over to the bar. I sit down at the bar to rest.

"You tired already?" Zayn says in jest.

I nod as I reach for my vodka soda, surprised to find a shot next to it. "You really got me a shot?" I ask.

He raises his hands in the air. "I did no such thing, swear."

The bartender says, "It's from that guy," and points in the direction of the bull-riding station.

My eyes search for anyone, and they stop when the older man with the braid tips his cowboy hat in my direction. I mouth the words "Thank you" as the bartender tells me, "That there is Frank. You impressed him, which is hard to do. Pretty sure you're the only gal who's ridden that bull in months."

My jaw drops and I look to Zayn.

"Look at you go, cowgirl. Summer must be so proud."

It warms my heart that he says this. She would totally love this story!

I raise the shot up in the air. "To Summer!" I down the shot quickly, grateful that it was lemon drop and not straight liquor. My throat burns.

At this point, I'm feeling a quite buzzed. *Ugh, I don't need another dumb night. I'm too old for this.*

He leans in close to me. "Uh oh. You doin' okay after that shot?"

"Yeah, totally fine," I say. I turn around but my foot gives out underneath me. *Shit, I better not break another bone tonight.*

Zayn's hands grab hold of my waist. "Easy there."

I blow out a breath. "It hurts."

"What hurts?" he asks. "Your foot?"

"Mhmm," I say nodding my head. "I think it's the same one I hurt before."

He looks around the bar still holding onto me. "Let's get you back on the stool for now. I'll check it out."

I nod as he guides me back down onto the stool.

"Cool with you if I take off your shoe?" he asks.

"Sure." I watch as he removes it and inspects my foot. One of his fingers grazes the arch of my foot and I let out a giggle.

His eyebrows raise as he looks at me. "Ticklish?"

"Yeah, a little," I say.

"Well, looks like you're good, but I do think we should head out of here and take it easy. You've had a lot of adventures for one night, cowgirl." He winks and smiles at me.

"On the house," the bartender interrupts and sets down another lemon drop.

I hesitate but reach for it anyway. I lift it into the air. "Painkiller, right?"

Zayn's about to snatch it from me, but it's too late. I down it with one big gulp. A tingle spreads throughout my body.

"That's probably the last thing you needed."

"It's fiiine," I wave off his comment.

His face grows stern. "Seriously, Autumn. I think we should head out now."

"Why are you worry—err worried about meee?" My words begin to slur. "Wait, wait, wait, mister! I...you owe me an expl—explanation. Damn it, you know what I mean. Is Riley's mom Sam or not?"

"Yes, she is," he says.

I blink several times with wide eyes, fighting the tears that are begging to escape. "So, is that why you stayed here? For Sam?"

"Absolutely not. It only happened because I was so broken and fucked up from my choice to stay here. It was honestly just a moment of weakness since I couldn't handle that I'd let you go."

The words spew like vomit. "But *Sam?* It just doesn't add up for me. Ugh. So grosssss."

"I get it, Autumn. I really do. We'll talk about it one day when you're not drunk. But, if there's one thing I can reassure you, I did not cheat on you or stay here for Sam. I never wanted anyone else. You were it for me."

Hearing those words, my eyes can't help but to fall to his lips. My body slowly starts to lean in. I'm dying to kiss him. Sirens blare in my mind. *No, no, no, Autumn. Do not do this! You're drunk!*

He gets closer to me. *Wait—do I want this to happen? What am I afraid of?* He is only a couple inches from my lips, when suddenly, it hits me. I stand with urgency, and my hand flies across my mouth.

I race over and grab hold of a nearby trash can. People surrounding the area realize what's happening and flock to the other side of the bar. There are a few people lingering around laughing about it, and a couple of others who are way too drunk to care.

When my hands release the trashcan, I lift my head to see the bartender pouring me a fresh cup of water.

"You might want to take it easy there, young lady," he offers, setting the glass of water next to me. He looks to Zayn and says, "You're driving her, right?"

"Oh yes, sir. For sure. I'll make sure she gets home safely. Thanks," Zayn replies as he starts to slowly rub my back.

He whispers in my ear. "Autumn, I'm sorry. I shouldn't have taken you here."

My head begins to pound, but after the release, I feel a little better. "No, it's fine. I've had a great time. But no more ssshots for me. *Ever.*" I grab a cluster of the tiny square napkins from the bar and use them to wipe my mouth.

"Not a bad idea considering the last few shots have really done you in." He says as he hands me a cup of water.

I take a few sips. "Oh, that feels so much better. Thanks."

He gives me a nod before thanking the bartender once more and we make our way out the door.

I stumble into his truck, and the feel of his arm holding mine sends electricity through me. His touch sobers me.

Once settled in, I slouch against the door and close my eyes. I feel somewhat embarrassed. *We were about to kiss and then I threw up. How disgusting is that?*

Once we're on the main road, Zayn turns down the radio and says, "Hey, you still awake?"

"Yeah, just super sleepy," I admit.

"Well, how about we cross one more thing off the WOLO list tonight?"

"Mhmm, okay."

"All right, hold on tight," he says.

His rickety old truck feels like it's flying.

"Autumn," he says excitedly. "We're doing a hundred miles per hour. In my truck! Woo, baby!" He pats the dashboard, and I can tell he's feeling proud that this old truck still has the capability to do this.

The adrenaline has us both reeling and once again, he looks like he wants to kiss me. *Maybe I'm imagining this?*

Zayn must have released his foot from the gas pedal because I can feel the engine slowing down.

"That was so much fun, Zayn. You're the best! Thank you for the best night ever!" I say like a drunken idiot.

He bursts out in laughter. "Wow, Miss Parker, now I know you're still intoxicated."

A few seconds later, he surprises me by taking my hand in his. He uses his left hand to steer, while holding onto mine with his right. Heat rises to my cheeks when he gives it a squeeze. I pretend to look out the window to hide the ginormous grin across my face.

We may have been driving a hundred miles per hour a few minutes ago, but the thrill of holding his hand after all this time gives me a rush like no other.

10

☑ Flash or Moon Someone… Again, Possibly

☑ Throw a pie in Mr. Parson's Face

I wake up in my bed, still completely dressed in my jeans and purple crop top. My clock on the nightstand reads 9:37 a.m. I can't remember the last time I slept in this late. College, maybe? Trying to remember the night, it occurs to me that Zayn must have put me to bed. I check the spot next to me to make sure I'm alone. A sigh of relief washes over me.

I head to the bathroom for my morning routine, hoping it helps with this hangover. I hop in the shower, ready to feel fresh after a night of bull riding, drinking, and sleeping in the same clothes I wore all night. The water wakes me up a bit more, and I take a moment to breathe in the scent of my new, relaxing lavender body wash.

Even after I've washed up, I take the time to stand there, enjoying the water running down my body. The shower can often be a sacred place for me to feel refreshed and relaxed. A noise from the living room startles me so I turn the water off. I stand in the shower for a moment, listening for further sounds. Nothing. *Phew, just my imagination.* Living alone has had its freedom, but I must admit it's added a new layer of paranoia to me with every creak and hum. And being right on the beach means constantly hearing the crashes of the waves and people talking as they walk by.

I step out onto the mat, wrap a towel around my body, and grab a second one for my hair. The mirror is steamed over, so I decide to go to the kitchen to start a pot of coffee before getting dressed. Before I can reach the kitchen, I'm stopped by the sight of someone on my couch. I scream for a second, until I realize I know this person. Zayn.

"Um, excuse me? What are you doing on the couch?" I say, demanding answers.

He rubs his eyes, more than a few times, as if he thinks he's in a dream. "Oh shit, I'm so sorry. You were pretty wasted last night, so I was worried. Plus, I was too tired to drive back to my place last night, so I crashed on the couch." He leans forward. "It makes sense you wouldn't remember."

My mind searches for memories of what happened. Everything seemed pure until I was hit with a memory of almost kissing just before puking into a trashcan. Yikes. "Yeah, I'm really sorry about last night."

"No apology necessary. But I am sorry about Sam. I should've told you I messed around with her after you left. I was a fucking idiot who thought sleeping with anyone would help me get over you."

"Glad we can agree on one thing."

His eyebrow arches. "Me being an idiot?"

"Yup." I exhale. "I guess it all worked out for everyone."

"Guess so." he says. Zayn sits up on the couch. The blanket he was wrapped in falls, revealing his bare chest. "For what it's worth, I had a great time last night."

His perfectly defined pecs serve as a distraction. It's hard for me to take my eyes off his chest. *What am I, a dude now?* Those pecs are seriously perfect, and his shoulders look even more muscular without a shirt on. I take in a deep breath. "Aside from vomiting in front of a bunch of strangers, I had a pretty good time, too." I head over to the counter to look at the WOLO list, grateful for the distraction so I can stop gawking at him.

We both look up from the list and at each other. He smiles wide showing his perfect teeth. I start to melt a little bit, feeling my face flush. My eyes fall to his chest and abs. He is even more fit than he was when we were back in high school. It's obvious he works out, which I want to tease him and roll my eyes at him for, but I stop myself. It dawns on me I'm still only wearing a towel. His lips part as if he's about to say something, but he holds back. I interrupt the moment. "I should probably get dressed."

"Uh, yeah," he says, heading over to the chair with his shirt. He tosses it on. "You get dressed. I'll make us a pot of coffee."

I nod and begin to turn around when suddenly my towel slips, revealing most of my boobs along with exposure of at least one nipple. A tiny scream evades me as I quickly pull it back up. My face turns beet red as I look to Zayn for his reaction. I catch him staring at me, mouth agape. "Please tell me you didn't see anything," I plea with embarrassment.

He clears his throat. "I uh—I saw only a little." His eyes meet mine but slowly make their way back down to my chest. Lust lives in them, and I can't help but feel flattered at his reaction.

"How does this seriously keep happening?"

He chuckles slightly. "I think it's safe to say you can't stop yourself from flashing and mooning me. Accidentally, of course." He winks at me.

"So not funny," I say as I slowly head back towards my room. "I'll be out shortly," I yell as I close the door behind me, secretly wishing I didn't enjoy the look on his face.

ONCE I'M out and fully dressed, I go to find Zayn. A pot of coffee sits on the counter with a note that he's sorry he had to go, but he got called into work. *Why do we both have jobs that never end?* Although to be fair, his is way worse since a fire can literally happen at any time and if he's on call, he's got to go.

Searching for my phone, I decide to call Mason and Natalie to see if they want to do something tonight. The three of us decide to hit up the Lake View Fall Festival held at the beginning of each fall season. I know it's lame, but for some reason, I've always liked this time of year best since my name is Autumn. I'll never admit that to anyone, though.

When we arrive, it's packed. Most importantly, Mason and I vent to Natalie that it's packed with . . . students.

"Oh well," I say. "We can still have a good time. Not like anything crazy is going to go down."

"Welcome back to a small ass town," Mason says before laughing.

Natalie rolls her eyes. "You guys are both so dramatic."

Mason wraps his arms around the two of us but looks at me. "Pretty sure, she just means me."

"Oh definitely," I tell him. Natalie shoots me a wink and a smile. It really feels good to be surrounded by my old best friends again.

"It's whatever. Now ladies, let's have some fun. What should we do first?" Mason asks.

Natalie points to the one thing I wish she wouldn't. "Let's do the Ferris wheel first," she says.

"Yes, let's go," Mason says.

I begin to pull back a bit. Natalie notices and asks me, "What's wrong?"

I sigh. "To be totally honest, I've never been on a Ferris Wheel. They sort of freak me out. What if it tips with us in it?"

"Wait, is it on your WOLO list with Summer?" Mason looks at me as hope fills his eyes.

I shake my head. "Sorry, but no."

"Oh okay, well no worries, girl. We can do something else," Natalie offers.

I start to agree when it hits me. The whole point of the WOLO list is to step outside of my comfort zone. To take risks, do things unplanned, and to stop being such a chicken about everything.

"You know what? No. Let's go. It doesn't matter that it isn't on the list. I want to try it. And who better to go with than two of my best friends?" I say. Mason and Natalie each grab one of my hands excitedly.

"Woo hoo!" Mason exclaims. "Let's do it for Summer!"

"Yes, for Summer!" I agree. We make our way to the line for it when I suddenly spot Summer's old nasty retail manager, Mr. Parson. "Ummm speaking of Summer, do you guys remember that asshole manager she worked for who told her she'd never amount to anything more than a cashier?"

Mason and Natalie both nod their heads.

"Yeah, why?" Natalie asks.

"He's right over there," I say pointing him out. "And you know what is on the WOLO list? Tossing a pie in that guy's face for all the BS he put Summer through."

Mason and Natalie exchange a quick glance.

"You don't have to ask us twice. Let's go find some pie!" Mason exclaims.

We begin a mission to find some pie, and luckily, at the fair, there is a literal pie-throwing booth. *Um, is this real? Can't get any more convenient than this.*

"Guys, look!" I shout. I quickly look around to see if anyone is paying attention before snatching a pie off the table. Mason and Natalie follow close behind me.

I let the adrenaline course through my veins as I walk at a fast pace over to where Mr. Parson is standing. When I've reached him, I stand behind him and say, "Excuse me— Mr. Parson, is that you?"

"Yes," he says turning around. Before he can make out who I am, the pie meets his face. The cream splatters on his neck and clothing, and we all watch, mouths agape, as the tin pan slowly slides its way down his face and falls to the ground.

"Sorry," I say instinctively. I blow out a deep breath and start to turn around.

I change my mind and spew, "Wait, no. I'm *not* sorry. That's for treating Summer and who knows how many other employees you've had, like garbage. That's for being the clown of a person you are." I kick the pie pan on the ground to add more of a dramatic touch before walking away, heading back over to Natalie and Mason.

Mason is clapping and doing a little happy dance and Natalie has her hand in the air, signaling a high five. "Girl, you are a queen!" she shouts.

I clap my hand to hers and smile. Breath flows through my nostrils as the adrenaline swims through my veins.

Mason puts his hand out for one too before saying, "I don't know what you've done with my best friend, but I'm not upset about this glow up, girl. You were such a badass. Summer would be so proud."

"Thanks, that means a lot," I admit feeling proud of myself, too. "Alright bitches, I'm feeling bold."

"Me too," Natalie says. "What do ya wanna do now?"

"Ferris wheel, here we come!" I shout.

AFTER QUITE AN EXHILARATING WEEKEND, I struggle to make it through the day at work. Somehow, I manage, but it doesn't make much of a difference since I have to stay until seven p.m. for Parent Teacher Conferences. Riley asked if she could stay in my room until conferences began, so I sent her to do a few tasks and errands for me in the library and front office. I begin tidying up and arranging the room for the parents.

Mason pops in the room to check on me. "Hey boo, how you feeling about tonight's conferences?" He looks around the room to make sure we're alone since he would've seen Riley leave the room not too long ago.

I let out a sigh of relief. "I think I'm ready for it. Just a bit nervous about you-know-who's conference," I admit.

Mason makes an awkward face and lets out a small chuckle. "Oh honey, I do not envy you. I think it'll be fine though. I thought things were good between you and Zayn though now, right?"

"Right, it's definitely been a nice surprise for me. But he

really isn't the one I'm worried about," I say. "In fact, he has to work tonight so he isn't even coming. It's just going to be Sam."

"Oh?" He arches an eyebrow before continuing, "Honestly, you'll be fine with her. I know her personality can be a bit crass and direct, but she's been so excited for you to come work here. She is different now, too. I wouldn't let her worry you."

"Thanks. Yeah, I think I just have to readjust to her personality. I don't want to have to keep avoiding her either," I say.

"You got this, boo! You're going to do great tonight. Come by my room or shoot me a text if you need anything . . . or need saving." Mason gives me a final wink and a wave.

"Thanks, Mace. See ya," I say.

I start stacking report cards and information sheets in order of those attending tonight when the door opens, and Sam enters the room. "Hey lady!"

"Oh, hey Sam," I say. I'm not sure why she's here so early.

"Sorry, I don't mean to surprise you with last minute changes, but I asked one of your parents to switch places with me so that we could meet first to chat before the rest of our conferences." *Damn, she is so bold.*

"Um, okay," I say as politely as possible.

"Is it, though?" she asks. "Is it okay?"

I allow myself a slow breath in through my nostrils, internally debating if I am okay with it. *Guess it'd feel nice to get it over with.* "Actually, the more I think of it, that makes sense. It's no trouble at all. Come on in and have a seat."

Sam comes over to the table and we both take a seat across from each other. "Thanks so much. You really are the best. I won't take much of your time, really all I wanted to do is see how Riley is doing, but also to tell you how much she's already blossomed this school year. She absolutely loves having you as a teacher."

"Thank you. It's been a pleasure having her in class. An absolute joy. She's helpful, inquisitive, and a quick learner," I say, speaking truthfully.

Sam smiles at my words. "Autumn, I can't thank you enough for making my Riley girl so happy. And her dad, too. Haven't seen him this happy since Tori."

I'm sorry, what now? Who the hell is Tori? I freeze, unsure how to feel about that comment.

"I'm glad to hear that Riley is enjoying class. And I'm grateful you and Zayn are such supportive parents. As you know, it makes a world of a difference," I say. To fill the silence, I hand over Riley's report card and review it with Sam. My hand trembles a bit as I start to review Riley's grades, but I'm hoping she doesn't notice.

After hearing about her current quarterly grades, Sam says, "Okay, well everything seems just as I thought with Ri. Thanks, Autumn."

"Sure thing," I say, standing up and pushing in my chair. Relief floods my body knowing I've made it through my first conference of the evening—the one I dreaded most.

Sam gets up and gathers the paperwork for Riley. Just when I think she's about to leave with a simple goodbye, she says, "Also, maybe it's not my place, but are you actually into Zayn or . . . what's going on there?"

I should've known better. I'm not in the clear just yet.

Without showing she's caught me off guard, I say, "Zayn and I are history. You know that." I squint at her.

"Well, I know how history can repeat itself. No hard feelings between us, right? Zayn and I were literally just a one-time thing. And I'm so happy I have Riley now, but that was definitely more long term than he and I had planned," she jokes.

I smile and nod. "I understand. And you and I are good."

"What a huge relief!" She flashes me a big smile before giving me a wink. "I do see the way he looks at you though."

I hold up a hand to cut off the conversation there. "I promise we're just really good friends now. That's all."

"Okay. Oh, and careful around Riley, too, please. She's noticed you two have spent quite a bit of time together, so I wanted to be in the know of what's been going on so I can be honest with her," she explains. She picks up her bag and turns to leave. "I guess it does make sense you two would be close again. Zayn was always helping Summer in her final days. I should've known he'd be the same with you."

I'm sorry, what? This woman is dropping bombs on me left and right. He took care of Summer, and no one told me?

"Alright, off to my conferences I go. Tootles, Autumn." She blows me a kiss before walking out into the hall, the door shutting behind her.

My feet don't move. I stand there shocked, trying to process all the new information I received. I'm sure Tori is no one, or else Zayn would've mentioned her. But he was with Summer in her final days, and no one bothered to tell me? I chew my tongue a bit, reflecting on how it makes sense now that he had the letters from her. He was there for Summer. That's huge. Massive. Someone other than Mom and Dad was there for her when I couldn't be. And of all people, it was Zayn. Maybe he has changed.

11
☑ Get High

The last kid of the day leaves so the other teachers and I make our way back into the building.

Sam matches her pace with mine. "How'd the rest of your conferences go last night?" she asks.

I smile and say, "All went smoothly. I'm just exhausted today."

She nods in agreement. "Yeah, I feel ya there."

"What about you? How'd they go?"

"All went well except one parent blamed me for her daughter's reading score dropping. So, that was fun. I think I'm reaching burn out from these past few years. Plus, my class size is now at thirty. I'm losing my mind."

My jaw drops at her words. I don't think I've ever related so much to her before now. I'll admit it's nice seeing this more vulnerable side of her. Maybe Mason is right.

I slow my walking and wrap my arm around her shoulders. "Sam, first of all, it is not your fault. Just remember, we're always the first to blame. Also, I've been feeling that exact way now too for so long. Burnout is real. And we're all expected to just keep going through the motions."

She stops and looks at me. "To be honest, I don't know how much more I can take."

"I know," I say wrapping her in a hug.

"Why does it have to be this way? And if I quit, Lord

only knows what the heck I'll do." Her voice shakes. "And I'm a single mom, so I don't have a choice."

I squeeze her tightly. "I'm so sorry." When I pull away, our eyes meet. The white around her eyes reddens and tears fill the corners. "Look, take it one day at a time. Something I'm learning is that if teaching isn't for me—although I don't think it's great for most nowadays—it's okay to try another career."

"Yeah, but I'm sure that's easier said than done. Especially with how much of my life I've already dedicated to teaching." Her voice shakes.

"Oh absolutely. That's why I decided to give it another shot down here. Which, I'll admit that a change of scenery has done me a world of good. So maybe you go to Cherry Blossom Elementary or try out middle school. No matter what you choose, just try to remember it's okay to change your mind."

Boy, do I wish I took my own advice. How do I always know what to say to others but can't figure out how to do things myself?

"Thank you, Autumn. I needed to hear that," she says.

A man's voice cuts in. "Hey, you two. Am I interrupting something?"

I breathe in a sigh of relief at Zayn's touch of my shoulder. I turn around and smile.

"Oh, we're just venting about this lovely job," Sam explains.

He nods. "Yeah, you guys have it rough and with such little pay. It sucks, I'm sorry." He shrugs. "You could always apply at the fire station."

Sam and I laugh.

"Well, I know one thing's for sure. I'd much rather rescue a cat from a tree than feel like I'm herding cats and being attacked by panther parents for eight hours a day," I joke.

"Girl, preach," Sam says.

"I take it last night with conferences was a bit rough?" Zayn asks as his eyes shift back and forth between us.

"Don't even ask," she says.

"I'll fill you in another time. It's finally Friday! Let's go out and celebrate," I say.

"That's why I'm here." Zayn winks at me.

Sam parts her lips. "On that note, I'll leave you two to it." She looks to me. "Thank you again for listening."

"Anytime," I say and wave as she heads down the hall.

I turn to Zayn. "Want to walk with me to my classroom so I can grab my stuff and we can grab a bite to eat?"

"Lead the way," he says.

When I open the door, I remember what a giant mess the kids left this afternoon. We got so busy with a project that the bell rang before we could clean it up. I walk over to my desk and grab my bag and phone before taking a final look around the room. I exhale loudly.

"Everything okay?" he asks.

"Yeah, it's fine. Let's go. This place is a disaster, but I need to quit sweating the small stuff. The kids will help on Monday," I say, trying to convince myself more than anyone.

"Yeah, it's been a long week for you. You deserve to not have to clean up after a bunch of children right now."

I nod and close the door behind me. *He's right. I'm so tired and this is a future-Autumn problem.*

When we reach the parking lot, I decide to ask the question that's been pestering me since last night. "Hey, how come you didn't tell me you helped Summer before she passed?"

His jaw drops open. "Oh, well, I figured it was the least

I could do after what I put you through years ago. Summer was a great gal, and I knew your parents would appreciate the help."

I stare at him.

"I actually used to ask her for updates on you since I felt like such shit for what I did. At first, she wouldn't give me the time of day—which I deserved—but I didn't give up. I think they figured I'd never let up on making things better, so she and your parents gave me another chance." His eyes soften. "When she started to have difficulty with chemo treatments, I stepped up and helped however I possibly could. It was nothing, promise."

"But it wasn't. It was everything, Zayn. Really," I say.

A second later, his arms are wrapped around me. Instead of resisting, I wrap my arms around him and allow myself to cry against his chest. "It means the world to me knowing that you did that."

"Hey, don't mention it. I heard through the grapevine that you had to stay in Greenwich except for a few trips you made, so I wanted to help."

I pull away and wipe the tears from my cheeks. "Ugh, I should've been here."

"Hey now, don't 'should' on yourself. Even if you had gotten down here sooner, you couldn't save her. You did your best, Autumn. And Summer knew that."

Perhaps, he's right. Even if Liam and I had moved back here, it wouldn't have kept her here any longer.

I nod. "Thank you for saying that. And for . . . all your help with Summer." I take a deep breath. "And it explains how you got the letters in the first place."

"Yeah. Sorry that was so confusing at first. I should've told you, but I knew you couldn't stand the sight of me at first."

"That is true. You really do like to wear people down. I'm glad Summer gave you another chance, though."

"I guess you could say I'm persistent. My guilty conscious is what prompted me in the first place, but nevertheless, I've got no regrets from it. Anyway, I'm off for the next two days, so let's take advantage of it. Why don't you come to my place tonight? I have a special surprise again."

I squint my eyes. "You and these damn surprises. You're starting to sound like Summer, or just a creepy guy trying to get me to get into your van for some 'candy' or something."

Zayn laughs and says, "Ha, sorry! I totally didn't mean for that to sound as creepy as it came out. I really do have a little bit of a plan if you want to come to my place."

"Fine, let's go," I say before wiping away any remnants of tears and giving him a huge grin.

I FOLLOW Zayn inside the house. I kick off my shoes by the door and set my crossbody bag on the couch before taking a seat. I grab a couch throw pillow—which the man has two of, shockingly—and sit cross-legged on his couch.

"Want something to drink?" he asks, heading into the kitchen. I look around the room and stop when I noticed the axolotl we painted together hanging in his living room.

"Just some water would be great, thanks," I tell him.

"You got it," he says. "Oh, and feel free to put on the TV if you want to watch something."

He heads back into the living room and sits next to me

on the couch. "Here's your water," he says setting it down on the coffee table.

I thank him and take a sip. When I set it back down on the table, I notice a brown paper bag and lighter next to him. He's staring at me, and my guess is he's trying to gauge my reaction.

I hesitate to react right away. Finally, I ask, "Um, is that what I think it is?"

He nods. "Indeed, it is."

It finally clicks. The WOLO list. "Wait . . . are we getting high tonight?"

Zayn shrugs before releasing a chuckle.

"Okay. Oof. I'm just nervous. Not sure if I'm ready for this, to be honest," I tell him.

"I mean, me neither really. I—I don't do this stuff, usually. I only bought it for us to do for the WOLO list. It's on there, remember?" he asks right as he grabs my hand in his. It sends a warm shock throughout my body at the very touch. I pause and stare at him.

"It's all right," he says. "We don't have to smoke it if you're not comfortable."

"No, it's fine. I am. I—" I bite my lower lip.

"What is it?"

I inhale. "It's just . . . well, Liam used to try to pressure me into trying coke with him all the time. He was big into it for a while, and I used to just ignore it. But then, the more we got to know people from his real estate business in Greenwich, I realized it was like all anyone ever did. I think sometimes people with money have too much time on their hands. But, I mean, I do think weed is fine. Not that I ever really get the chance to get high," I explain.

"Yeah, I get that. Right after high school, I'd get high at parties. Preferred it to drinking. But, damn, after seeing the shit my dad has done and put us through with his addictions, I just don't find any of it worth it anymore," he tells me.

He slouches back and leans against the couch. "I feel that you should know, but I stayed here for my dad. I wanted, and tried my hardest, to help him. But hell, not long after my dad found out about Riley, he made all sorts of threats to me, told me I was gonna be a shitty dad, just like him." Grabbing the remote from the coffee table, he puts on a random show to have something on for background noise. I notice a tear run down his cheek.

"Zayn, I'm so sorry," I say, placing my hand on his shoulder. "I can't believe you never told me that til now. I never understood what made you stay here. Thought you fell in love with someone else. Not to mention, Sam just tossed around the name Tori at Riley's conference."

Tossing the remote back onto the table, he leans back against the couch, waving me off. "Pfft. Tori is no one. Just a girl I never should've dated for as long as I did. I promise it wasn't serious. At least nothing compared to you and Liam."

His words simultaneously provide sting and comfort.

"Well, that's a relief. Did you ever love Sam?" I ask.

He shakes his head. "You know, I'm not sure. It was just a fling to try to get over you."

My cheeks flush. "I definitely thought you got over me way sooner."

"It was so long ago. Back when I really would just use girls. All of them, but you," he says.

I want to melt from his words. But do I believe him? "Mhmm, sure," I say, scoffing. "So, you didn't love her? You didn't really answer."

He clears his throat. "I, uh, I think I loved—still love— her for the mom she is to Riley. But never in love with her, you know? Even though there were times I kept trying to be with her to do the 'right thing'—whatever the hell that is." He lets out a laugh.

I laugh too, feeling more relaxed after finally hearing the truth.

"And," he continues. "I should've told you I was only staying for my dad, but I really didn't know how. I was young and dumb and trying to do what's best. I stayed for my dad originally, but it worked out because I couldn't imagine life without my Riley bug. So, I decided if I were gonna be stuck in this damn town, I'd be different. I'd be a good dad."

My body naturally scoots closer to his. "I know I've said this before, but you are a great dad, Zayn. Riley is an amazing young lady, and we both know I'd never give all that credit to Samantha," I joke.

He manages a smile. "Ha, ha, thanks. I guess."

"I hate to admit it but seeing you as such a good dad has shown me that you really have changed. For the better. It's so nice to see."

"That means a lot to hear from you," he says.

We both get silent for a moment.

"I realize I haven't asked, but how is your dad doing now?"

He leans back. "Ehh, I couldn't tell you. We hadn't spoken in a few years until the other day before our night at Daisy's Roadhouse. He stood in front of my truck, wanting to talk to me. Make things right."

"Oh dang, I'm sorry. I assume things aren't good between you guys then?"

"Nah, I cut ties with him since he was never sober, always getting arrested, tried setting our house on fire a few times, and I could never trust him around Riley. Ever since we lost my mom, he's thrown in life's towel. And now he wants me to just forgive him. Give him a second chance.

But I don't think that man has ever loved or cared about anybody. Not even me. I stayed for a man who wouldn't do the same for me. And at what cost? I lost you."

Tears begin to flood in his eyes. "Shit, I'm so sorry," he says, using his thumbs to wipe at his eyes. "I, uh—I'll be right back."

I watch as he stands up from the couch, heading toward the bathroom. Without another thought, I stand up and grab ahold of his forearm.

"Zayn, wait," I say, turning his body around to face mine. We stare into each other's eyes for a moment, but then I fall I embrace him in a big bear hug. It's like putting on my favorite sweatshirt.

I whisper, "I'm so sorry." Slowly, I pull away and place my hands onto each of his upper arms, gripping him tightly. One hand drops and I take hold of his chin, directing him to meet my eyes.

"Look at me," I say breathily. "It's all gonna be okay. We're okay. I wish you had told me this before. And look at us now . . . Zayn, you haven't lost me. I'm still here, but as a friend instead."

He exhales. "Thank you."

"It's nothing. And hey, for what it's worth, maybe consider giving him a second chance. I'm slowly learning people really can change, for the better." I say with a wink before grabbing the bag of weed from the coffee table.

"All right, enough with the mushy gushy stuff. We gonna get high or what?"

Zayn bursts into a fit of laughter, and I'm so excited for what the night has in store for us.

"Whoa, this list is changing you, Miss Parker."

"It really is," I say handing over the bag to him. I'd prefer he be the one to get the party started.

He nods before taking a seat back on the couch with

the bag in his hand. Peering inside of the bag, he quickly crinkles it back up and sets it down between his legs before whipping his head back and releasing a loud sigh.

"Oh no, what's the matter? Is there no weed in it?" I ask.

He tries to cover a chuckle with his hand, but I can clearly see a giant grin plastered across his face. He laughs. "Well, it's not even a joint. It's gummies."

"Ha ha, for real?"

When he finally calms down, he says, "Technically you and Summer did only add 'Get high' to the list, so it still counts, right?"

"Hmm. I guess that's true. Do they even work though? I've never gotten high from any smoking, so gummies seem like . . . I don't know, some kind of joke, I guess," I explain, realizing I have no clue what I'm talking about. All those years spent hanging around affluent people who smoked and drank, and yet here I am with the street knowledge of an elementary schooler. And even they probably know more than I do nowadays.

"It sure seems like you're doing a lot of guessing. Here, check them out," he says, handing the bag over to me. I peek my head in the bag before reaching for the package of gummies inside.

I hold them, analyzing the package and the picture of them on the front. "They look like some knock-off version of Starbursts or something."

He leans forward. "You're right. They do!"

I open the box and pull a couple out. They really do look like giant Starbursts.

"Okay, so, you ready?" He asks, grabbing one from the palm of my hand.

"Ugh, I don't know if I can do this," I admit.

"Nerves getting the best of you, huh?"

I nod my head. "Yeah. What if I get out of control or

hate the way I feel? There are so many things that could go wrong. Maybe this will be the one adventure I can't do."

"Don't let your anxiety get the best of you. I promise you, it's just one gummy. Plus, you're with me. We're gonna be fine. You might end up falling asleep from it anyway," he says.

"I—I guess I'm just a little scared." I blow out a deep breath. "You're right, though. One gummy for Summer. She probably would have had me smoking joints with her every time we got together if I'd ever caved to her wishes."

Zayn nods. "Your sister was quite the partier, wasn't she?"

"Oh yeah, definitely."

"She was never obnoxious about it, though. She really was such a free spirit," he notes.

"Ha, for sure. She was the best sister. Never pressured me even though I know she always wished I was more adventurous like she was," I explain. "I mean, sure, she'd give me a hard time, but she never fully judged me for not being a huge partier and risk taker like she was."

"Nah, she liked you just the way you were. It was always obvious to everyone that you two completed each other," he says.

I flash him a slight smile. "Yeah, she really was the yin to my yang. I guess it's not so bad to have one little silly gummy for her. Let's do it."

We each hold a gummy up to our mouths.

"Wait," he says. "I just want to say one last thing. I really don't know why I never told you the truth. I guess perhaps I thought you'd think I was using my dad as a lame excuse to not be with you. Which looking back on it, maybe it was." His gorgeous brown eyes lock into mine.

"I appreciate that," I say.

He clears his throat and I'm hoping this gummy helps

me get out of my own head about Zayn. I cannot fall for him again.

He continues, "Anyway, thanks for listening and for being so forgiving. You're one of the best people I know, Autumn."

"I should be thanking you too. You've helped shake me out from my comfort zone, and I've honestly enjoyed it . . . a little bit, anyway." I wink at him. "And this is me admitting this before the gummy starts talking."

We both crack up.

Zayn lifts his gummy high and mighty into the air and says, "Cheers to us and our first adventure with getting high from gummies."

A smile crosses over my face. "Cheers."

12

I glance away from the TV. "Well, shit. Maybe it didn't work. Are you feeling anything?" I ask Zayn.

"Hmm . . . not really. Should we try a second one?" he asks.

I shrug and pull the bag back closer to us. "Let's do it. It's been half an hour and nothing. What have we got to lose with trying a second?"

"Your call, Miss Parker."

"Let's do it," I say with fake confidence; I'm actually scared shitless of getting high. Zayn doesn't seem to notice my hands shaking with trepidation, so I feel like maybe it's all in my head. *Maybe getting high will be good for me with this damn anxiety. I'm so sick of overthinking and worrying about every little thing, every single day.* I exhale deeply before I pop the next gummy in my mouth. I notice that Zayn does the same thing. Maybe he's nervous, too.

"This has been such a vulnerable night for me, I could really use a good high," he says. I couldn't agree more.

I nod before scooting closer to him on the couch. I didn't realize how close I got until I breathed in a huge whiff of his cologne. Or maybe deodorant? Either way, it smells so sexy. I take in a second subtle sniff before I scoot a bit further away from him. I want to make sure that if I do get high, I don't do anything stupid.

Speaking of stupid, my text message alert goes off. I grab my phone from the table and look at the screen, shocked at the name that appears. *Liam.*

"What could he possibly want?" I ask aloud, cueing Zayn to look at my phone, too.

"Uh oh. That can't be good, right?" he asks.

"Yup," I say while setting the phone back down. "It's fine, I'm going to ignore it. I'll check it later."

Zayn gives a subtle nod and looks back at the TV. I wonder if it's just as obvious to him as it is to me that neither of us has actually paid any attention to the show. I don't mind the distraction of being here, though. I've never been to his place before, but I do oddly feel comfortable being here. Maybe it's simply the feeling I get whenever I'm around Zayn. Not that I'll admit that to him, of course.

I start to smile, lost in thought, when Zayn interrupts. "Autumn, check the message. It's killing me to see what he wants."

Ooh, what am I sensing here? Is he perhaps a bit jealous? Or maybe he's just this nosy now. "Yeah, you're right. I'll check it quickly. What on Earth does he even want?"

I swipe to unlock my screen and click on Messages. I decide to read it aloud:

Liam: I have some news. Can you talk for a few?

"What would he have to tell me that's news?" I shrug. "Ugh, I should probably give him a quick call and get this over with. What do you think?"

Zayn's mouth falls open, but only nonsense sounds come out until he finally says, "Uh—I . . . don't know." I look at him longer waiting for a better response when he suddenly bursts out into uncontrollable laughter.

"What is so fun—?" I begin to ask, but I'm cut off by the sound of my own obnoxious laughter. I cover my mouth to suppress it. This makes Zayn laugh harder and soon enough, the two of us are rolling on the floor, hands pressed against our stomachs in a fit of laughter. After what feels like several minutes of pure, insane laughter, I sit up to ask. "What was I even doing?"

Zayn shrugs, and we both continue giggling. He then rolls his body upward to a sitting position. "Autumn, I have the *best* idea," he tells me.

"What? Tell me now," I demand.

He then stands to his feet and offers his hand down to me. I accept without hesitation as he says, "Let's go. We can walk from here."

Once to my feet, I still feel the warmth from his hand and realize I haven't yet let go. He must realize it, too, because he lets go and forces his hand to comb his hair back. I watch as his fingers move through each strand in seemingly very slow motion. My gaze breaks when he asks, "You ready?"

"I guess so." I grab my phone from the table and stick it in my back pocket. "Should I bring my bag with me?" I ask as he tosses on a hoodie. I put my sweater on, too.

"Nah, it'll be a quick walk, and I've got my wallet," he says patting the pocket of his jeans. My eyes quickly shift from the pocket to the bulge next to it. I can't help but wonder if the bulge is always there or if . . .

"Come on," he says, grabbing my hand again. The electricity that jolts through me feels dangerous yet comforting.

We start walking down the street, both attempting to hide our highs from one another. He keeps sneaking glances at me. Of course, I only know this because I'm doing the same thing to him.

"So, how do you feel about tacos?" Zayn asks me, breaking the silence and shared stares.

"I love them," I say. "I'm so glad we're eating. I'm freaking starving."

"That's perfect," he says as he leads the way across the street. I'm focusing on his butt in those jeans when he finally stops abruptly in front of me. "Hope you're ready for the best tacos of your life."

My eyes fall to the hideous truck with a sombrero on it. "Pedro's Tacos?" I read the words off the side of the truck. "You've got to me kidding. We're eating tacos from a food truck. That sounds to me like a recipe for instant diarrhea."

Zayn shakes his head and releases a chuckle. "Even high as a kite, you're gonna be feisty, huh?"

"It's not being feisty if I'm simply speaking the truth," I say matter-of-factly. A puppy-dog look flashes across his face as his eyes widen. "Oh dammit, don't give me that adorable look. You look like the cat from *Shrek.*"

"Adorable, eh?" he teases. "Look, all you gotta do is at least take one bite, so you can officially say you've had food from a food truck. If you hate it, you don't have to eat it, and I'll order take out from somewhere else. Deal?"

I cross my arms dramatically for a moment. "It is on the list, at least. And I'm definitely feeling a slight buzz, so maybe this is the best time to try it. Plus, I'm starving. I bet anything will taste good right about now."

Zayn walks up to the truck and orders for us. It's nice being with someone who's a lot more down to earth. Not that I'm *with* him. Even when I'm high, I'm not crazy enough to fall for someone again. Yet here I am, crazy enough to eat tacos from a food truck. I shrug. *Guess it can't be any worse than Taco Bell, right? This is for you, Summer. I miss you.*

I'm pulled from my thoughts when Zayn walks back to me with two paper baskets of tacos. "These are for you," he says, handing me one. With his free hand, he motions to a bench near the sidewalk.

Once we both take a seat, I watch him take a bite first.

"Don't tell me you're backing out of this now, are you?" he asks.

"Nope. Well, maybe. I'm waiting to see if you get sick or die first," I tease.

Zayn smirks before saying, "There's that drama queen I know so well, making her appearance. I've been wondering where she went. You've been quiet lately."

I elbow him playfully in his side and he lunges forward, dropping the taco in his hand. Zayn and I both stare down at the splattered taco on the sidewalk. My eyes shift back up at him to witness the disappointment washing over his face. "Oh my gosh, I'm so sorry!"

"It's all right," he says, acting nonchalant. "I'll get a new one in a bit. But first, you should make it up to me. Eat one of yours!"

"Fine, fine," I say, picking up one of the tacos as he watches me on the edge of my seat. I take a bite slowly, trying not to show emotion. With each crunch of the taco, I taste an avalanche of flavor. The seasoning is hands-down the best I've ever had. I close my eyes to savor the taste.

Zayn gasps. "You like it, don't you? I see the truth all over your face," he exclaims.

I hesitate to answer in my reluctance to prove him right. I hold out my pointer finger to signal I need to finish the bite. He scoffs.

"All right, fine. You caught me. It's delicious," I admit, taking another bite.

"I knew it!" He says as a smile spreads across his face as he watches me take another bite.

In between bites, I ask, "You're not going to sit and watch me eat all night, right?"

He chuckles. "Nah, sorry. I'm just so excited that you're enjoying them. It's nice to see you so happy." He pauses before adding, "I'm gonna go grab myself another one. Want anything?"

I shake my head and focus on enjoying every bite of the taco until my phone vibrates my entire back pocket. Shifting to the side, careful not to spill the rest of my tacos, I pull it out. I see Liam's name flash across the screen, but this time it's a phone call. *Shit.*

13
☑ *Dance in a Fountain*

I set the plate down next to me on the bench and my eyes find Zayn at the truck. I gesture to him that I have a phone call. He gives me a nod to take the call. I swipe my thumb across to answer.

"Hello?"

I hear Liam's quick sigh. "Hey, Autumn. It's Liam." My eyes roll at the obvious, but I decide it's best not to say anything snarky like I usually would.

"Hi Liam. Sorry I hadn't responded to your text yet. I've had a busy day," I say staring at Zayn with a smile.

"Oh, it's not a big deal. I'll make it quick. Just wanted you to hear it from me first, but . . . well, I'm engaged."

I begin to choke. "I'm sorry—what? Did I mishear you?" My eyebrows make their way up my forehead as I look at Zayn like I can't believe what I just heard. He mouths a "what?" but I just shake my head in response, signaling he's never going to believe it either.

"Uh, no. I'm engaged. To a woman named Leah actually. I realize it seems pretty quick, but as they say, when ya know, ya know, right?"

I freeze as I'm brought back to awareness, feeling completely sober. What a literal buzzkill Liam continues to be, even after our marriage. I realize I should probably respond so I exhale and say, "Wow, that's awesome. Congratulations. Wishing you both the best of luck." All these years in customer service and teaching, I've definitely learned how to feign happiness. Internally though, I can't help but think, *sorry, what? How could you? What an asshole!*

"Uh, thank you, Autumn. I really felt it best that you'd hear it from me first," he says.

"Understandable. I appreciate that," I tell him. *Do I, though?*

"Cool. Well, I'll talk to you later."

"Sounds good. Bye," I say and hang up right before the floodgates of my eyes open to release all the pent-up tears. I let them flow and place my head in my hands.

As I start to ugly cry, I feel Zayn's hand on my back. "Rough call, huh?" I hear him ask me.

My tears continue to rain down on my hands for a few seconds longer before I finally wipe them away. A shaky, deep breath escapes my lips. "Yeah, it was Liam." I pause to swallow before adding on, "He called to tell me he's getting married." More tears try to break through the dam, but I force them back and look up at Zayn.

He leans in and gives me a big squeeze, his arms feeling like a weighted blanket. Closing my eyes, I allow myself to breathe in his dark, woodsy scent. *He smells so good.*

Zayn interrupts my thoughts when he clears his throat and says, "Shit, Autumn. I'm so sorry. I don't really know what to say." He slowly releases me. I want to tell him—beg him—not to let go, but I stay silent. I lunge forward a bit, longing to feel his arms again. Fortunately, my mind resists the urges my body keeps having.

I shrug. "It's fine."

"Autumn, don't be silly. It's not fine. You two just got divorced a few months ago and he's already engaged to someone else? What a dick move! That's unbelievable." Zayn stands up, his brows furrowed. He puts his hands in the pockets of his hoodie.

"I—I just don't even have the words. He clearly cheated

on me or at least moves on super fast. Screw him. He's such a jerk!" I allow the anger in me to come out through my words.

I pick up my last bit of taco from the plate next to me. "What you don't know though is . . ." I leave him on a mini cliffhanger to take a bite of the taco. "Liam and I have really been going through the motions for quite some time. Even if he didn't cheat on me, I can see why he's moved on so quickly. For the past two and a half or three years, we were basically nothing more than roommates who argued all the time and sometimes went out together." It shocks me that I finally admitted those feelings after all this time of suppressing them.

"Oh, really? I had no idea things were that bad with you guys," he says.

"Well, how could you know? How could anyone? I've been living all the way out in Greenwich for quite some time now," I say. Then it hits me. My sister must've told him about us. A debate of whether or not to ask him about it starts playing in my head. I cave in. "Did Summer ever talk to you about me and Liam?"

He looks away for a moment and runs his hand through his hair. "Um, yeah . . . she did. I asked about you a few times since you left. Never wanted to pry, since I knew if you ever found out I was asking about you, you'd probably hire a hitman." His eyes meet mine and we both smile. This simple exchange between the two of us sends a tingle through my body. "Anyway, why don't we get you back home?"

I nod in agreement, reaching for the final bite of the taco and savor it. I rise to my feet and bring my paper basket over to the trash can. When I head back to Zayn, I realize I'm not yet ready to go home.

"Would it actually be alright with you if we keep

walking a bit more? I want to clear my head and stay outside for now," I explain.

Zayn looks a bit surprised but doesn't question me. "Sure. Let's head this way," he says, gesturing toward the right of us.

I agree and we start to walk side-by-side along the sidewalk. Our hands occasionally brush against each other's, and I find myself wishing he'd reach out and grab mine. The news of Liam must be affecting me pretty bad if I'm even considering allowing Zayn to touch me. Again.

He starts to ask, "So, what do you . . ." but his voice trails off. I follow his gaze forward to a fountain in the middle of Sand Dune Park. How have I forgotten about Fish Fountain? It's been a landmark here since before I was born, and Summer and I with our friends used to come down here and hang out on the park benches near it all the time. In fact, it dawns on me that Zayn and I once walked past it on a date in high school. We both tossed pennies into the fountain and made wishes. Mine was *I wish to be with Zayn forever.* Hah. That one clearly didn't come true.

I shake my head, trying to escape the memory and notice Zayn looking at me. "Hmm, instead, I'd love to offer you the chance to complete one more item from the WOLO list for the night. You game?"

I contemplate it for a moment. I am getting tired, but I'm enjoying Zayn's company more, and now I'm about to be able to check off yet another item on the list. "Why not," I agree with a smile. "Let's do it."

We both start to run towards the fountain at the same time. "Last one there is a rotten egg!" I yell out to him as if I'm one of my students. He pauses and flashes me a goofy grin. My heart beats faster, and it's not just from the running.

As we approach the fountain, he looks at me while

whipping off his socks and shoes. I do the same. "You meant last one *in* the fountain is a rotten egg, right?"

"Sure did," I say, stripping off my socks and rolling up my pants to my knees. Zayn does the same. I take off my sweater as he his hoodie off, tossing it on a bench nearby. Despite the chill in the air, the adrenaline that pumps through my body warms me. As we continue to race, my eyes squint at him and he does the same. Reaching the fountain simultaneously, we both put one foot in the water. It's freezing cold.

"Wow, I didn't expect it to feel *this* cold," he admits, hesitating to put his other foot in. I nod my head in agreement.

Once both of my feet are in, I start to dance. Zayn smiles and begins swaying from side to side with his hands on his hips. "Oh my God, you're embarrassing."

"Oh, you mean when I do this?" He starts to do the Sprinkler and makes a squirting noise.

I snort from laughter. Trying to get a little deeper, I stop when the water hits my knees. "I think I'm getting used to the cold, except I'm definitely getting the mist from the fountain all over me."

"Oh yeah?" he asks, splashing me with a little bit of water. "How about now?" he teases.

I gasp. "What? You jerk!" I put my hand in and begin splashing him back. He tries to dodge the water by moving more towards the center, but his head ends up right under a fish spouting water and his hair gets soaking wet. I burst into laughter.

"Oh, I see how it is. Is that funny to you, huh?" he asks playfully while brushing soaked hair out of his face. I focus on bending down to get him even more wet with another big splash, but I'm thwarted by a face full of water. I shut my eyes instinctively and yell, "Hey now! That was—" I lose my balance and fall backwards. Water splashes all around me as my butt hits the bottom of the fountain. I open my eyes to find the water up almost to my neck. My whole body is frozen, and my eyes widen to look at Zayn, who is staring at me with his jaw open. It's obvious he thinks I'm pissed.

"Oh no, Autumn. I'm so sorry!" He comes closer to me, offering his hand to me. Instead of using his hand to help me to my feet, I flash him a mischievous smile and yank him in. He thrashes into the water next to me. Seeing him soaking wet and realizing we both probably look like a bunch of kids right now, I can't help but laugh. Zayn lets out a chuckle and admits, "I should've seen that one coming." He grabs onto one of the fish and pulls himself up. This time, he offers me his hand, but says, "I'm already wet, so this is your final offer, Miss Parker."

I grab hold of his hand, allowing him to pull me up. Stumbling to my feet, I don't let go of his hand until we're face to face. I almost fall once again, but this time, my hand falls upon Zayn's shoulder as I attempt to catch myself. It works and my eyes quickly shift to his face. My eyes widen and my lips part when I see the seriousness that's taken over in his deep, brown eyes. My gaze can't help itself but to fall to his lips, and my head starts spinning when I notice they're moving towards me. I close my eyes and allow his lips to take hold of mine. I'm soaking wet and freezing, but his mouth is warm, and his lips feel like pillows against mine. I turn my head, allowing his tongue to meet mine. The kiss feels both electric and familiar all at once. And I swear I'm floating in this fountain.

14

Toilet Paper Nick Hartzell's House

ayn pulls away from me, gauging my reaction. My jaw drops. I'm torn between wanting to kiss him again and slapping him.

"Was that okay?" he asks.

I nod, probably looking as giddy as a little kid in a candy store. I bite my lower lip in protest.

"Okay, good. I want to make sure you feel comfortable enough to tell me if not. Like, if it's not cool, I get it. Let me know, and I won't do it ag—"

"Zayn," I interrupt. "Just shut up. It's fine. Now kiss me again." Instinct takes over and I grab his collar, pulling him in.

The taste of his mouth is magical—a combination of minty and sweet. I move my fingers through his wet hair, catching a whiff of his fresh shampoo as if he'd just stepped out of a shower. His hands make their way to my midriff, rubbing slowly. I tremble, dying for his fingers to explore further. I'm aroused and filled with warmth despite being freezing a second earlier. His tongue exits my mouth, and he bites my lower lip with a low growl. I breathe out a slight moan.

Someone in the distance yells, "Hey, you two get out of the fountain!"

I pull away from Zayn, eyes wide.

"Oh shit," we both say in unison, hopping out of the fountain. We quickly grab our belongings off the bench and make a barefoot run for it.

Once we make our way around the corner onto another street, we pause to catch our breath in front of a closed-down Blockbuster. "You okay?" he asks.

Laughter takes over. "Yeah, I'm fine. I forgot we were in a fountain, honestly, til that guy hollered at us."

Zayn grins from ear to ear. "Same here."

"So should we get dressed and call it a night for real this time?"

He nods before saying, "Let's head into a convenience store real quick and dry off a bit."

"Good idea," I say. I start to think about how I haven't lived here in over a decade, and shouldn't recognize as much as I do, but the roads are as familiar as if I never left.

Once inside, we make our way straight back to the bathrooms, trying not to draw any further attention to ourselves.

"Okay, meet me back out here when you're done?" I say before ducking into the women's restroom.

"Will do," he says heading a bit further down the hall.

In the restroom, I head over to the hand dryer, standing directly underneath it and allowing the hot air to blow over me. I'm slightly tempted to put my mouth under here to see if I can make it look all crazy weird, but I probably shouldn't. *Wait, am I still high?* The thought crosses my mind. *Was I ever actually high?* My mind starts to wander to the phone call with Liam right before the fountain kisses with Zayn. *That was real, right?*

Someone walks in so I decide I'm probably as dry as I can be, and I make my way back out into the store.

I notice Zayn up near the register in line.

"What are you doing?" I ask, eyebrows raised.

He smiles. "Oh, nothing. A little shopping."

"For toilet paper?"

What a weirdo. "Did they run out in the—ohhh! Wait! Are we going to toilet paper Nick Hartzell's house tonight?"

"WOLO, right?"

"Ha ha, for sure. Let's do it," I say, hoping to hide how excited I am to spend more time with him. That kiss was just . . . everything.

Zayn purchases the toilet paper, and we begin walking towards Nick's house. We pass by a huge oak tree. Not just any old tree, but *the* tree. The one where Zayn and I shared our first kiss. We had been at a party at Nick Hartzell's—our unofficial second date. We had only gone to dinner once before, and I remember thinking he was probably going to ghost me. But, a few days later, he invited me to a party at Nick's.

I remember feeling like an outsider, surrounded by nothing but drunken girls and loud football players. Zayn held my hand the entire time and introduced me as his girlfriend. Sure, it was presumptuous, but my heart was thrilled.

After about an hour of uncomfortable meet-and-greets with people who I already knew (but who didn't know me), Zayn felt my discomfort and asked if I wanted to go for a walk. We were hand-in-hand when I first learned that Zayn was the boy whose house burnt down only a few blocks over from where I grew up. There were rumors that it had been a couple of neighborhood kids messing around, but Zayn told me he was almost certain it was his own father. I remember wrapping my arms tightly around him to comfort him.

"It's fine," he'd told me. "The minute I'm done with high school, I'm out of here."

"Your dad that bad, huh?" I asked.

He shrugged.

I remember looking at the oak tree before he said, "Want to run away together?"

"I think I like walking better," I said teasingly, my arms still holding onto his.

"Deal. Let's *walk* from this town and never look back." My palms were drenched with sweat. Knot in my throat. Warmth flooding my body as he leaned down and kissed me. We ended up spending the next two hours making out right there at the base of the old oak tree.

Zayn clears his throat. "Almost there," he says, interrupting my thoughts. "You doin' okay?"

I release a deep breath. "Oh yeah, I'm fine. Just zoned out for a bit."

"Mhmm," he says before his eyes shift to the oak tree.

We make our way up to the Hartzell residence, holding a bag of toilet paper rolls. "Um, how sure are we he still lives here?" I ask.

"Oh, I'm sure. He keeps trying to invite me over, just because we played football together when we were kids. With how he treats women, Hell would have to freeze over before that happens," he explains. "Any time I see him, he reminds me he still lives in the same spot and to come by anytime."

I watch as Zayn conducts a brief check to ensure no one is outside watching us.

"Coast looks clear. You ready Miss Parker?"

"Wait," I say, placing my hand on Zayn's and stopping him from pulling a roll out of the bag. "Does he still live with his parents?"

"Nope, just him. His parents left for Europe shortly after high school and let him have the house. I think they can't stand him just the same as everyone else."

"Oh okay, good." I pull out a roll and hand it to him before grabbing another for myself. "Um, one more question . . . we just throw it at the house and the roll does the rest of the job, yeah?"

He laughs. "Ah, my sweet innocent angel Autumn," he teases. "I forgot for a second you've never done this. But yes, aim high and throw. We gotta be quick about it too so he doesn't wake up and come out and bust us. Got it?"

I squint my eyes at him and scoff. "Just another virginity of mine you're taking."

Zayn busts out laughing. My face beams. It feels so good to make him laugh.

"Shhh," I say with my finger pressed up against my mouth. "Always gotta be the loud one."

I watch as his lips part dramatically. My mind briefly wonders if I should drop this toilet paper and kiss him again.

"Hey now. Am not!" he teases back.

"Okay, are we going to do this or what?" I ask, trying to snap myself back to reality.

We both decide that on the count of three, we throw as hard and as much as we can, and as soon as the rolls are gone, we're running back to his place.

"Alright. Ready? One, two, three . . ."

I can't believe it's already Monday again. Things with Zayn have at least given me a nice break from the Sunday scaries. Although, I've been so paranoid about getting arrested after toilet papering Nick's house.

This town is so small, I'm shocked there weren't any witnesses.

Before the WOLO list, our senior year of high school, there was a night of pranks that everyone was invited to participate in. Summer tried to convince me that they hadn't gotten into any trouble when she'd done it as a senior, but I wasn't willing to take a risk. While I knew then it was harmless, I still never wanted a chance at trouble.

It hits me that I've spent almost my entire life until now rarely taking risks. *How boring am I?*

"Ms. Parker, who's next?" A kid shouts at me, pulling me away from my thoughts.

"Oh, um, let me see here," I say looking down at my notepad with the list of student names on it. "Riley Mitchell."

Riley stands up and grabs a poster from her cubby. As she begins to walk up to the front of the room to share her thoughts on why she should be elected for student council this year, she looks directly at me.

"Uh, Ms. Parker, can we chat in the hallway really quick?" Her Zayn-like eyes stare at me.

"Right now?" I ask.

"Yes, please," she says.

This isn't very much like Riley to ask. I hesitate for a moment. "Uh," I clear my throat, trying to gauge whether the other students can handle this. "Sure, but just for a minute." I stand up and announce to the class, "Alright everyone, please share with your table partner who you feel has the most persuasive argument so far."

I cross my fingers knowing damn well that chaos will probably ensue the minute I step into the hallway with Riley. But she needs me, or else she wouldn't have asked.

She makes it out into the hallway first and faces the door.

Propping the door slightly open with my foot, I whisper to Riley, "Everything okay?"

She sighs. "Ms. Parker, I don't know if I can do this. What if no one likes what I have to say? What if I forget what I'm supposed to say? So, is it too late to change my mind? Can I back out?"

Ah, anxiety. My dear old friend. "Okay, first thing, I want you to take a really deep breath in through your nose and release it through your mouth. Let's do it together," I suggest.

We both inhale simultaneously through our noses before pushing it out through our mouths. "One more time," I say.

"Wow, that actually helped more than I thought it would," Riley says.

"Right?" I ask. "I was so shocked the first time I did it, too. But I've had anxiety pretty much my whole life, so I get that it's more than just presentation jitters."

She nods and looks right at me. "My chest feels so . . . I don't know."

"Tight?" I ask.

"Yes. I really feel like I can't do this," she tells me. Her eyes show a glimmer a fear and sadness. "I'm just gonna embarrass myself."

I place my hand on her shoulder. "Well, I'm certainly not going to pressure you into doing something you don't want to do."

She nods.

"But I know this is something you *do* want to do. You've been talking about it for weeks, and not just at school. Your dad told me this is something you've wanted to do since fourth grade. Is that true?" I ask.

My hands fold delicately in front of me, awaiting her response. I peek through the door to make sure the classroom hasn't escalated into a brawl or caught fire. It sure sounds like it has, but that's the case no matter who I'm speaking with. The president or a famous celebrity could come talk to me and the class would still go buck wild in the middle of our conversation.

Riley exhales loudly. "Yeah, Ms. Parker. That's true. I really want it, but—"

"Then don't let anxiety and nerves get in the way. Riley, I believe in you. You are brilliant, talented, and from what I've learned through similarities with me, prepared. Let's take some more deep breaths and get you back out there, hmm?"

"Okay. You're right. And yeah, I've been planning out my speech for a while," she says.

I smile. "You can do this, Riley. Give it your best shot. And remember, I'm here for support."

Riley flashes me a big grin before hugging me tightly. "Thank you, Ms. Parker."

We both head back into the classroom and the students fall silent.

"Alright everyone, Riley's up next and she's ready to go!"

The class cheers. I watch as she heads up to the front of the room for her speech. I notice she's taking in some deep breaths. When she's done, she looks right at me and smiles.

I gather my notepad and take a seat. My phone vibrates next to me, so I peek at the screen quickly. It's a message from Zayn.

ZAYN

Don't forget about me on your blind date this week.

Oh wow, I totally forgot I'm supposed to do that this week. I stare at the message a second longer. My heart does a back flip and a butterfly flutters around in my stomach. I turn my phone over and glance back up to Riley, reminding myself to not get distracted. I give her a thumbs up and she begins.

15

☑ Go on a Blind Date

"We're coming over," Mason says to me on our FaceTime call with Natalie.

"Definitely," Natalie agrees.

I glance in the mirror, scoping out the dark jeans and black top I have on. "You guys can just meet me there; I think I look fine"

"Honey, absolutely not. No questions asked. We'll see you in fifteen," Mason says.

"Alright, fine." I hang up the phone and head back over to my closet to see if anything new jumps out at me. I haven't been on a real date in years. Hell, since I first dated Liam. And now here I am about to go to dinner with a guy I have never met before. My breathing begins to shorten, and I feel my chest tighten. "Go away, anxiety!" I yell out to myself in the mirror from the closet. *Deep breaths.. It's fine. It's one date.*

I decide to check on Quinton while I wait for them to arrive. Picking him up, I bring him over to my chest. Sure, he's not a cuddly pet, but he's low-maintenance and chill. While petting him, I hear a knock on the door. Before I have the chance to set him down, Natalie and Mason have already let themselves in. My lips form a smile as I shake my head at how comfortable they both are with me even with all this time apart.

Natalie sets down her bag on the kitchen counter and spots me in the living room holding Quinton. "Oh my god, Autumn, I can't believe you're going on a date tonight!"

Mason laughs as he plops himself down onto the couch. "I mean, she's kind of already been on dates . . . with Zayn."

"Zayn and I aren't dating though. Well, honestly, I don't know what we are right now."

"Oh yeah?" Natalie asks. "Give us the deets, girl!"

"Not too many deets," I admit. "But we've kissed twice now."

"Oh wow, I for sure saw this coming. Zayn has always been your kryptonite," Mason says.

"No, he hasn't! Anyway, I think he's really changed so we're just sort of friends for now," I explain.

"Yeah, friends with benefits," Natalie adds. "Although, Mace, let's give our girl more credit. She's changed, too. I mean, Autumn when you left for NYU, you said you'd *never* move back here, you'd *never* get divorced, and that you'd *never* give Zayn the time of day again," she says.

"Yeah, I was super resistant to everything at first because, well . . . I despise change. Okay, despise is a strong word, but I'd say it definitely makes me feel uncomfortable. I like plans and predictability."

"We know," Natalie and Mason say in unison. We all laugh, and it feels like old times. It's funny how with true friends, so much time can pass and yet it feels like no time has passed at all.

"So, why are you going on this blind date tonight?" Natalie asks grabbing my hand.

I take in a deep breath. "It's on the list and honestly, I feel like it's something I need to do. What if Mace is right and Zayn is my kryptonite? Maybe I need to explore my options a bit more even if I really don't want to. I'm definitely nervous." Checking my watch, I realize I have only about thirty minutes left until he comes to pick me up.

Mason must've checked the time too because he jumps up from the couch and says, "Well, it's settled. Autumn, it's only one date, not a wedding." He looks over to Natalie. "Let's get our Cinderella ready for the ball!"

Natalie clasps her hands together in excitement. "Yay!" she squeals.

"Okay guys, follow me. I definitely need help picking out an outfit."

Mason looks me up and down and grabs my hand. "Oh yes, you really do."

After about twenty minutes of me modeling different outfits, we all agree on a little black dress that I haven't worn since one of my first dates with Liam. "I can't even believe this still fits me," I tell them.

"You look damn good too, girl!" Natalie says.

"Autumn has always been known to pull off any outfit," Mason says winking at me.

"Thanks, guys. I haven't felt like myself in a while so this is bringing up my confidence a lot. Thank you." I look at myself in the mirror. Natalie comes over with a pair of jeweled stilettos Liam bought for me in Greenwich Village. Mason hands me a pair of earrings, also from Liam.

"Wow," I say, putting on the shoes and earrings. "So much of my stuff came from Liam. He was definitely trying to dress me up more than I ever realized."

Mason gives me a big, bear hug. "Oh Autumn, remind me and we'll take you on a shopping date soon. You deserve it. After losing your sister and getting a divorce all within a few months, you need some retail therapy, my love."

"Not sure how much we can afford on our salaries," I say to Mason.

"I've got some money saved for these types of emergencies." He winks at me.

"Emergencies, huh?" I ask.

"Yes, boo. It's an emergency because you haven't treated yourself to something in who knows how long, and as one of your long-time best friends, I can't allow it. It's an emergency."

"Fair point," I agree.

Taking a final look in the mirror, I hear a knock on the door. "That's him. You sure I look okay?"

"Breathtakingly gorgeous!" Mason says.

"Yes, girl," Natalie agrees. "You're a babe in that dress. He probably will want to take it off you the minute he sees it."

I wave off her comment and head to the door. I open it to find a tall, attractive man with bright blue eyes.

"Damn, you must be Autumn," he says.

"Yup, that's me. Adam, right?"

"You got it, little miss." He smiles and something about it feels untrustworthy.

"I'm just about ready," I say, taking note of his suit and tie. Thank goodness I didn't wear jeans. He compliments how nice I look, and I tell him the same before inviting him in to meet Mason and Natalie.

As he chats with them, I recognize that suit. It's the same one Liam wore on that day in the coffee shop—when I found his divorce papers.

Adam interrupts my thoughts and asks, "So, you ready, beautiful?"

Brushing my hesitation away, I respond, "Yes. I'll grab my coat and bag, and we'll head out." I turn toward my friends and wave. "Please lock up when you leave. We'll see you guys at the party tonight."

"See ya," they say, waving us out the door.

Heading out to his car, I notice it's a Porsche. His eyes meet mine and he smiles. Something tells me he's hoping I comment on the nice car, but I don't. He opens the passenger door for me, but his eyes don't leave my body until he shuts the door. I buckle my seatbelt as a chill shoots down my spine. As he puts the car in reverse, he says, "So, nice car I got, huh?"

Ew, gross. I nod my head, mustering a fake smile. "Definitely," I say, shifting in my seat. I can't help but think about how much I'd rather be in Zayn's beat-up old truck right now.

He only talks about himself the entire way to the restaurant. We drive to a nearby town, and I begin to question if I'm about to be murdered in the woods right now. The valet service opens my door and I step out on the brick pavement. I haven't worn stilettos in a while so this seems a bit dangerous.

Adam comes over and puts my arm through his. He smiles and tells me this is his favorite restaurant. Of course it is. I want to roll my eyes, but instead, I exhale and think to myself, *maybe tonight will go better than you think. Give him a chance.*

Once we're seated, he immediately has a bottle of wine sent to the table. He still hasn't asked me a single question about myself, so I decide to just get to know him more.

"So, Adam, I know through some of our texts you mentioned a successful business you've created. Very impressive. But, what about you, personally? What do you for fun?" I ask.

The server comes over to pour our wine into glasses. Adam takes a sip, and then tells him, "We're ready to order."

"Oh, let me look really quickly," I say. I haven't even had a chance to look at the menu. As I rush to glance it over, he tells the server, "I'll have the steak and lobster, and she'll have the salmon salad."

Excuse me?

I hate salads. I start to speak up to say, "I'd actually like—"

"Thank you, sir, that'll do." Adam flashes the server a grin and he's gone before I can squeeze out another word.

I cringe when he says, "Trust me, you'll love it." My mouth is agape, but Adam doesn't seem to notice, or care. He starts to answer my original question. "I do go out a bit with some of the guys from the office. We take fishing trips once a month, and I do enjoy golfing."

"Oh, that's great," I say.

"Yeah, I also love going to this one bar, The Rabbit Hole. You ever been?" He asks without even looking at me. I turn my head to see what has caught his attention. This time, I do roll my eyes when I find it's a tall, skinny blonde chick with cleavage for days. I try not to compare myself, but damn, it'd be nice to have his eyes on me—his date— right now instead. Perhaps that's asking for too much nowadays. "No, I haven't been." I don't even follow up with any more questions. If he wants to get to know me better, he can be the one to start asking questions.

The food arrives at our table. Adam looks over at my salmon salad and says, "I should've gotten that instead. Looks delicious, am I right?"

"Would you like to trade then?" I offer.

"Oh no, I'm not much of a salad guy. More of a surf 'n' turf, so this plate is much better for me. Thanks though."

He's got to be kidding. If only I wasn't raised to be so dang polite. I want nothing more than to get up from this table, toss my glass of wine all over his Liam-replica suit, and walk away without looking back.

But what do I do instead? I sit there like a rock that can't move while dying on the inside. I decide to eat only the salmon of my salad and down as much wine as possible. The waiter offers dessert, and right as Adam is about to order, I interrupt with, "Oh, actually, we're both on a diet, but thank you."

The server gives a smile and a nod before announcing that he'll be right back with our check.

Adam stares at me blankly. We both sit in awkward silence until the bill arrives. If I had to guess, he's giving me some type of silent treatment since I spoke up for the first time all night. *This guy's a real winner.*

He pays the bill and says, "Well, you're welcome." *Unbelievable.*

"I do appreciate the dinner, but I can speak for myself."

He gets up and offers me his hand. "You're right. My apologies. Let's blow this popsicle stand and get to the party, hmm?"

I hesitate to respond. He notices and follows up with, "Come on, Autumn, what do you say? Give our night out a second chance?"

I've tolerated him this much. I figure it can't get much worse, right? "Sure, sounds great," I say, hoping I don't regret it.

16
☑ Crash a Wedding

Zayn's eyes instantly meet mine from across the room. Of course he's here. Even when I'm at some random dude's house party. I'm unsure if people are just soaking in the nostalgia of the decade before or if they actually believe they're still in high school. Yuck. Sometimes change is good.

I smile and give him a little wave. He waves back right as Adam steps in front of me.

"Who the hell was that?" Adam demands.

"A friend, if you must know," I snap back. *Why did I think it was a good idea to come to a party with him? The dinner was bad enough.*

"Well, allow me to make some friends," he says as he grabs hold of a random girl's hand and swirls her around.

He whistles, and the girl eats it up as if he's the best thing since sliced bread. I want to vomit. "I—uh, excuse me," I say.

The girl begins grinding on him to the music. "Hey, now I'm finally getting a little somewhere tonight." I watch as he licks his lips.

And . . . I'm done.

My tongue wretches out as if I really might lose my salmon salad, and I head out for some fresh air.

When I reach the front porch, I see an old wooden swing. I glance around, checking to make sure I'm alone before taking a seat on it. The older I get, the more I lose the need to be surrounded by a sea of people all the time.

The swing reminds me of the one at my parents' house. I close my eyes, breathing in the salty air. My thoughts fly to Summer and the time we'd spent reading or talking on the porch swing, sometimes arguing over what we should do next. The slight ocean breeze blows my hair behind me. I smile. I really have missed this place.

"Hey," a voice says. "Where's your date?"

I open my eyes and scoot over for Zayn to sit next to me on the swing.

When he does, I explain, "His name is Adam. He's still inside actually. Hitting on some girl."

"No way." His hand makes a tight fist.

"Yes way." I wave my hand in front of me. "It's fine. He reminds me so much of Liam. Well . . . worse, actually. So, I'm not even that upset to be honest."

"Yeah, you definitely don't need another douchebag in your life. You do seem to attract them, though."

I elbow him playfully. "I sure do."

"Oof. I walked right into that one, didn't I?"

We both laugh, and he puts his arm on the back of the swing. As if on cue, I lean back into the crevice between his arm and chest.

He uses his legs to keep us in motion and we sit in silence together on the porch while the music from the party thumps.

An idea strikes. "Hey, want to go on a WOLO adventure?" I ask.

His lips part and eyebrows raise. "Right now? Are you sure?"

"Yeah. You in or what?" I stand up from the swing, extending a hand for him.

"Sure, I'm in. What'd ya have in mind?" he asks.

I walk away, pulling him behind me. "It's a surprise. Tell ya when we get there." I pause to look at him. "Wait, are you cool to drive? I don't have my car. Adam drove us here."

"You know I'd drive you anywhere, anytime," he says pulling out his keys from his pocket with his free hand.

"Perfect. Then you drive, and I'll tell you where to go."

He follows my command with no questions. We hop into the truck, and he starts the ignition. "Alright, missy. Tell me where to go."

"OKAY, TURN LEFT HERE," I direct to Zayn. Checking the time, I see it's already after midnight.

"Alright, turn right here," I say.

He makes the turn. "So, are you going to tell me why we're going to the Friedman House? I thought you could only get in if you had a big event booked or something."

"Hmm maybe we can find parking over there," I suggest. He drives his truck around the grass parking lot of the house, searching for a parking spot.

"This place is packed. Is it your parents' anniversary party?" He manages to find a spot and pulls in. "Yes! Found one." He turns off the truck's engine and looks at me. "You going to tell me what kind of event this is or what?"

"Come on, loser. No time for questions. We're already late. Let's go," I say, hopping out of the truck and closing its door behind me. Zayn follows my lead as I head towards the live music.

"The band is good," he says, practically yelling to make sure I can hear him. I watch him as he moves his head along to the beat, swaying his shoulders to the music. *He really is so cute*, I admit to myself. *Just friends, Autumn. Just friends.*

We finally reach the large gazebo that's attached to the historical home. My eyes glance over at Zayn to see if he's figured out where we are yet.

"Wow, it's gorgeous," I tell him, mesmerized by the twinkling strands of lights hanging above the dancing crowd.

"Well, this is quite the party," he says. "Wanna dance?" He extends a hand to mine, palm up.

I grit my teeth. "Ummm, I'm not sure about that. I'm pretty clumsy."

"Me too, but who cares? Everyone's too busy dancing and having a good time to notice us. And if they do, we will totally rock it as the goofy couple of the evening." He raises his eyebrows and flashes puppy dog eyes at me.

"Fine." I accept his hand and follow his lead out onto the dance floor. I don't know the song, but it's a catchy enough beat to do my usual hip-swaying and shoulder-shifting, one-arm-above-my-head dance move on repeat. I started dancing like this in my college days, and I don't think I've ever done a different move since.

Zayn's goofy dancing is so adorable that I can't help but laugh.

He points at me and says, "You laughing at me over there?"

"I might be," I tease. Sure enough, he starts mimicking my moves. A loud laugh that hurts my cheeks erupts from my mouth. "You can't imitate these suave dance moves of mine," I say. I start dancing emphatically, attempting a twerk.

"Oh, we twerkin' now, are we?" Zayn places his palms down on the wood floor of the gazebo and shakes his booty like Miley Cyrus on stage in 2013. A crowd forms around us, clapping and cheering him on.

Tears of laughter stream down my face. I bend over, clutching my stomach as cramps settle in. "Zayn!" I yell, half embarrassed and half impressed.

He comes up from the floor and tosses his sweaty hair to the side. Completing ignoring the crowd surrounding us, he asks, "Don't lie. Wasn't that the best twerk you've ever seen in your life?"

I laugh, struggling to catch my breath. I shake my head and say, "I truly cannot take you seriously right n—"

"Oh my God," a voice from behind interrupts me. "Well, if it isn't Autumn Parker!" I turn around. She must be able to see the guilt written across my face. "What the hell are you doing here?" The music quiets and the room pauses to focus on us. Me. Zayn. And the angry bride I've pissed off by showing up uninvited.

"Oh, uh—hi, Veronica," I say while awkwardly giving a tiny wave. "Congrats?"

Veronica steps toward me and Zayn in her white wedding dress. "You. And Zayn Mitchell . . . really?" Her eyes narrow in disgust. Veronica waves a hand in the air. "Ugh, whatever. Both of you need to leave. Now." Her hand makes her way to her hip, indicating she's waiting for us to leave any time now.

Zayn tosses his hands up in the air in total innocence. "Veronica, you do look lovely." He then looks to the groom. "Best of luck to ya, man."

I grab hold of one of Zayn's hands and, together, we flee the dance floor. I let him take the reigns as we navigate through the crowd. The feeling of the eyes of everyone in the room remain upon us. We reach the couple of steps, leading us off the porch of the house and make our way back out into the dark parking lot, which is only lit with one fading streetlight and the stars above.

I let go of Zayn's hand and rest it across my chest. When I catch my breath, I tell him, "Sorry about that. Maybe it wasn't such a good idea to crash Veronica's wedding."

"Not a good idea," Zayn says in between breaths. "It was the *best* idea you've had yet! The look on that bitch's face was priceless, Autumn."

"I know, but I feel bad. I'd have been pissed if someone crashed my wedding. That's why I thought we'd play it safe with one of your friends' weddings," I joke.

"Yeah, my friends would've just offered us a round of drinks on them. They're very laid back." He tells me as we walk closer to the truck. "Honestly, this was a good call. Veronica was so rude to everyone in high school, but especially to you. She had it coming."

I'm shocked by his words. "You noticed how bitchy she was to me back then?"

"Oh yeah, for sure. It was totally uncalled for. I hope she's changed now or else that guy is in for a not-so-great surprise," Zayn says.

I nod my head in agreement. "You know, when you say things that way, change really isn't always so frightening."

He looks at me with wide eyes. Cupping his hands around his mouth, he begins to shout into the abyss of the night. "Ladies and gentlemen, I present to you . . . Autumn Parker having a breakthrough. A true epiphany. She sees the bright side of change!"

I smack him on the side of his shoulder. "Shut up," I say.

He smirks. "You really have changed a lot, you know? In a *good* way, Autumn. Change can be good."

"Yeah, I guess you're right. Change can be good, but it still makes me anxious. We can't all be Mr. Easy-Going, living a life free from anxiety," I say folding my arms across my chest.

"That's fair. Also, you know I'm not completely flawless, right? I'm trying to practice not projecting my own worries and insecurities onto Riley, but I can't even trust her to light a candle in her bedroom." He shrugs. "We're all fighting our own demons every day."

"You can say that again. But I don't know if I'd trust any kid with a lighter and that's coming from someone whose house has never burned down," I offer with a slight chuckle. "That said, Riley is so smart and responsible. You're doing great as a dad, Z."

He pauses for a moment and leans back against the bed of his truck. "You know I used to like to plan things out too. But you learn to be flexible real quick, especially after becoming a parent, and even more so when you're a kid yourself."

He pushes himself away from the truck and tucks a loose strand of my hair behind my ear. With one simple touch, my entire body ignites with excitement.

"I'm sorry I've been so resistant to change since I've been back," I tell him.

He waves my words away. "Oh, but Miss Parker, that's not the case at all. All you've done since you've been back is step out of your comfort zone. I'm proud of you. And you've trusted me, even when I least deserved it."

"Well, I am only using you to complete this list, ya know?" I tease.

"Oh, trust me, I know. Deep down inside of you, I know that change-hating, untrusting, sarcastic Autumn awaits her return the minute we're through with the WOLO list." He bites his tongue playfully.

"As long as you already know, then we're good. We

should always be on the same page," I say, sticking out my tongue at him.

"Speaking of, now you get to cross off 'Crash a wedding' from the list. Job well done," he says.

"I thought you'd agree," I admit.

Zayn looks at his watch. "Hey, it's pretty late, and I know we both have work this week. Let's get you home."

I nod. He holds open the passenger side of the door for me and I climb in. I buckle up as he walks around to the driver side. When he makes his way into the truck, I say, "Hey, thanks for tonight. Despite watching those God-awful dance moves of yours, I had a good time at Veronica's wedding."

He smiles. "Thank you for the awesome night, too. Pretty sure Veronica's already thinking of leaving her husband now that she's seen my twerking," he jokes.

I laugh again as he throws his truck into reverse. "You're probably right," I say.

"And it just got even better. Autumn Parker tells me I'm *right*. Doesn't get any better than this." He squeezes my knee with his hand.

I smile and think to myself how happy I am when Zayn's around. Maybe it's time to quit resisting it so much.

17

☑ *Go Camping at Cherry Springs*

☑ *Cliff Dive Off Sunrise Rock*

We arrive at Cherry Springs and try to find the camping spot our friends are at. When we finally spot them, Zayn pulls the truck up in the grass and looks at me before tossing it into park. "You doin' okay?"

I look out the window at the campground. "Honestly, camping is not my thing. I'm terrified of bugs, creatures, wildlife, and well . . . all the things. I think maybe 'glamping' is more my style."

He chuckles. "Think about how brave you've already been, though. You're doing great with the list, A."

I sigh. "I know, I know. You're right. This is definitely me overcoming my fears though for sure. But two nights here? We should've started with one."

"Think of it this way—I know you're on fall break, but I'll probably get called into work anyway, and then it'll all end early," he offers as consolation.

"You're not just gonna leave me here, are you?" The

very thought prickles the tiny hairs on the back of my neck.

"Absolutely not. I was trying to offer that to give you some potential relief to your anxiety, not to make it worse. Come on, let's do this." Zayn hops out of the truck and waves to our friends on his way over to my side of the truck. He opens the door. "Mason and Nat are here, too by the way."

"They are?"

He nods. "Mhmm. I convinced them to come. We both know if we can get someone like Mason to go camping, you'll do just fine."

I laugh as I grab his hand and step down from the truck.

We walk over to the center of the campsite spot while he holds the small of my back.

I see Ryker's already grilling some hot dogs and hamburgers. He yells over to us, "You guys hungry?"

We exchange a quick glance. "Starving," I say.

"Yeah, me too. Need any help over there, bud?" he yells to Ryker.

"Yeah man, that'd be great," he replies.

Zayn looks at me for approval and I nod before heading over to take a seat on one of the folding chairs next to Mason and Natalie.

"Well hey there, fellow camper," Mason sings.

Natalie hands me a drink. "White Claw?"

"Sure, thanks," I say, grabbing a can.

A thin blonde comes out from behind one of the tents that's already set up.

"Hey babe," she says to Ryker, wrapping her arms around him. Zayn and I exchange glances and I wonder what he's thinking. Are we dating now? We're definitely in a weird gray area. I still don't think I'm ready to date, especially after Liam and that awful Adam guy. But those kisses we shared flood my mind every night.

"I didn't know Ryker had a girlfriend," I say.

"It's new," Natalie says, giving me the sense that she's not thrilled about it. She and Ryker were into each other years ago, but neither one was bold enough to ever move it beyond—well, whatever they are.

"That's Taylor from school," Mason explains. "Remember her?"

"Vaguely," I say, taking a swig from my drink.

Another girl comes out of the tent. She's blonde as well as lanky and wearing a tube top with shorts. Her hair is like a mountain of gorgeous curls that rests above her head. She heads right towards us.

"Yo, dude, pay attention! The hot dogs!" Ryker shouts at Zayn. Before I have a chance to glance back over to them, the girl holds out her hand to me.

"Hey ya'll. Nice to meet you. I'm a friend of Taylor's," she says shaking my hand.

"Hey, I'm Autumn," I say.

The blonde offers her hand to Natalie next.

"Tori."

She makes her way to Mason, who says, "Great to meet you, Tori."

Tori. Tori. *Tori.* My mind rewinds itself to parent teacher conference night when Sam dropped that name so nonchalantly. *Is this the same girl? Zayn's . . . ex?*

My cheeks flush as I hope I'm assuming wrong. It can't be her.

"Well, can't wait to spend time with y'all. I'm gonna go see what the guys are up to," she says heading over to Ryker and Zayn.

I hop up swiftly and make my way over to them as well. Nonchalantly, of course.

Tori squeaks, "Hiii Zayn-y baby! Need a hand?"

I cringe. A knot makes its way from my stomach to my throat.

"No, thank you, Tori. We're all good," he says.

So, he's brushing her off. That's a good sign, right?

"Dinner's ready, y'all," Ryker shouts out to everyone. I get closer to Zayn and grab two bags of chips. I start opening them and bringing them over to the long picnic table that's been set up.

Mason and Natalie make their way over to the table while Tori and Taylor take their seats. The boys bring over the burgers and hot dogs. Taylor points around the items on the table, ensuring all the condiments are there before setting down a stack of paper plates. I sit next to Natalie, leaving room on the end for Zayn.

Tori notions for Zayn to sit next to her just as Taylor announces, "Alright everyone, eat up."

Zayn plops a burger onto the empty bun on my plate before taking his seat next to me. I let out a sigh of relief before grabbing the ketchup. He smiles. After I've finished reaching for the condiments and stacking chips onto the plate, I'm met with his hand on my lower back. My body feels like it's on fire and it's not just this North Carolina heat.

He leans in close to my ear and whispers, "Want to share a tent with me, Miss Parker?"

My eyes widen with excitement. I guess I didn't really consider the sleeping arrangements, but it does make the most sense for me to bunk with Zayn. Natalie must have heard him; she nudges me with her elbow.

I clear my throat. "Um, yeah. Sounds great."

He smiles.

"Well, under one condition," I add.

He closes his eyes and shakes his head. "Always a condition. I wouldn't expect anything else."

"You have to make sure it's bug free before we go to sleep. Deal?"

Zayn laughs. "Bug free camping? I'll see what I can do."

I nod. "I'm trusting you with this one, Z."

He winks and I glance a final time at him before taking a giant bite into my burger. *Maybe camping won't be so bad after all.*

ZAYN PULLS his truck up to a well-known cliff, Sunrise Rock—a huge tourist destination for cliff-diving. I think it's roughly thirty feet tall. This is one on the list that I'm most terrified of. Well, this and getting a tattoo.

"You ready to do some cliff diving?" Zayn asks me.

I exhale loudly. "Ah, I don't know. This is one of the top scariest things for me on the list."

"Don't worry, Autumn. I'm with you," he assures me, grabbing my hand in his and kissing the back of it.

"We are, too," our friends start shouting from the bed of his truck, which they all pile into. I laugh. I can't believe it, but I feel more at home here than I did my whole life I had planned out in Connecticut.

We all hop out of the truck and start heading toward the cliff. There are a lot more people here than I anticipated, and I'm not sure if that comforts me or makes me more nervous.

Zayn and I walk closer to the edge and peer over it.

"Whew, that looks steeper than I remember," he says.

"Wait, have you done this before?" I ask.

He nods as our friends gather around us, peeking over the ledge too. "Yup. Right, Ryker? He and I used to come out here all the time, dive off it, and swim for a while."

"Good times for sure," Ryker replies.

I take relief knowing they've done it quite a few times already. I look to Mason and Natalie. "What about you guys?" I ask. "Ever jumped this?"

Natalie looks at me. "I haven't, but I've always wanted to. I'm a bit scared, too."

"I've done it a few times, but it's been a while," Mason shares. "I'm also almost thirty, though, so I feel like I won't be able to handle an accidental belly flop as well as I used to in my teens and early twenties."

"Fair point," Zayn says to Mason.

"Mhmm, that's true." I take a final look over the edge and take a deep breath. I walk a few steps back and Zayn follows.

He asks, "So, what do you think? We doin' it?"

What would Summer say to me right now? I think about it for a while. I know she already would have dived in and come back up, begging me to join her in the fun. Or, like she said in her letter, that even as her ghost self, she'd remind me I'm still alive, and *we only get one life . . . don't waste it being too afraid to live.*

"Autumn, are you doing okay?"

I'm brought back to reality. "Yeah, sorry about that. I was just thinking about what Summer would say. I'm ready. It's now or never, right?"

Zayn nods in agreement before asking, "Want me to jump with you or do you want to do this on your own?"

I look around to see how everyone is starting to jump in. "Umm . . ." Before I can further debate this question, Mason and Natalie start running together.

"Cannonball!" Mason shouts as he tucks his legs against

his chest mid-air. In contrast, Natalie spins through the air like a ballerina as the two of them completely disappear over the cliff.

I run over to see if they've made it safely. I search for them in the water to find nothing, but then a few seconds later, I hear Mason yell, "Yeah, bitch! We did it!" The two of them high-five each other in the water.

"Come on, Autumn. You can do it! We're here waiting," Natalie shouts up to me.

I make my way back over to Zayn. "Okay, let's do it together."

"Alright, whatever you need," he tells me.

He grabs ahold of my hand, and we walk slowly up to the edge.

"Count of three?"

I grit my teeth. "Sure."

"Autumn, don't forget . . . Summer is with you and so am I. It's gonna be okay," he says as a final reassurance, which I didn't know I needed until he said it.

"Thank you."

"One, two, threeeeee—"

I close my eyes and leap into the air. I keep them closed all the way down, too afraid to see what's beneath us. Losing my grip of Zayn's hand, I begin to flail my arms in the air, trying to summon my inner bird. Just as I'm about to hit the water, I plug my nose and my feet hit first. The cold temperature sends a shock through my system. Within a couple seconds, I'm completely submerged and thrashing beneath the water. I hold my breath but force my eyes open underneath the water to see how far I am from the surface. It looks to be roughly ten feet. I quicky close my eyes and focus on large strokes to reach it.

When I finally do, I find myself searching for Zayn as I gasp for air. "Zayn?" I shout breathlessly.

"Hey," he calls out. "Behind you."

I swim towards his direction, trying to avoid the surrounding tourists. As soon as we're close enough, I pull myself up onto him and kiss him. He takes my legs and wraps them around his under the water.

"What was that for?" he asks.

"For helping me be brave. Again."

He looks down from my lips. "Autumn, don't freak out, okay?"

"Oh my God, what is it? Is there a bug on me?" I press my hand against my chest and back away frantically. Looking down, I notice my top is missing.

My eyes widen and I slowly look up at Zayn. "What the hell? Am I topless right now?"

"Uh, yeah," he says. "It must've come off when you hit the water."

"This cannot be happening right now." I start freaking out and swimming around in search of it. "What if I don't find it?"

Zayn shrugs. "I don't know. No, it's fine. We're gonna find it. Let's swim over to Natalie and Mason. Maybe they can help us look."

"You've got to be kidding me." I let out a tiny scream. "I'm glad the water is dark because at least no one can see me topless, but I can't see shit."

"Yeah, it's gonna be difficult. How about you stay here for a moment, and I'll swim over there to look."

"Okay," I agree. "Hurry, please!"

As Zayn swims off to find my top, I continually look across the surface to see if I can spot it. It's seriously nowhere in sight. After a few minutes of searching, Zayn returns to me.

"I'm so sorry, I can't find it anywhere."

"What do I do? Walk back to your truck topless?" I ask, secretly hoping this is all a joke.

He gives a half-smile. "I'm not sure what other option we have."

I take another deep breath. "Okay, let's swim close to the embankment at least." My mind starts spiraling and I try not to have a panic attack. *What's the worst thing that will happen? The answer is that maybe twenty or so people will see my boobs. Life will go on after this.*

We get closer to the embankment and Zayn pulls my hand for me to float closer to him. He holds me in the water. I can't imagine how much willpower this man has to have. He's practically naked with me once again, and there's certainly no promise of a happy ending.

"Okay so what's the plan?" I ask him, hoping he has one.

"I—I don't know. Let me think on it for a moment. I did tell Mason and Natalie, by the way. They laughed for a minute, but they're trying to find it."

"Great, I'm never gonna live this down," I say closing my eyes.

Zayn laughs. "I did tell them that every time you're with me you end up topless and wet."

I splash water at his face. "No, you didn't!"

"Ha ha, okay, you're right. I didn't. But it does seem like an odd coincidence that it keeps happening. I'm starting to think this is some big plan of yours."

I scoff. "Absolutely not. I'm mortified and you're over here cracking jokes on my behalf."

"Autumn," he says, moving closer to me in the water. "In all seriousness, I'm feeling a bit protective. I don't want anyone else to see you topless."

My body engulfs in flames at his words. I like that he's protective of me. I also took note of his use of *anyone else* to see me. Only him. Is it wrong that I don't mind he's seen my boobs so much now? Before more inappropriate thoughts creep into my mind, I see a purple bikini top floating next to him.

"Oh my God, Zayn! There it is!" I squeal in excitement and swim towards it. "I'm so relieved." I swim back to him and ask him to help me get it back on. He hesitates for a moment, but then agrees.

He ties the halter top around my neck as I hold onto the cups, then tries to locate the strings for the back underneath the surface of the water. His hand grazes my breast gently and my cheeks flush with excitement, but he remains focused as he finishes tying the strings around my back. I adjust the front to make sure the cups are secure and turn back to look at him.

"Thank you, thank you, thank you. I can't even believe that happened."

He flashes me a sweet smile showing off his pearly whites again. "I can't either. I'm glad we found it though. Well, somewhat glad," he teases.

"Let's get back to our friends. I've had enough excitement for today," I tell him.

"You and me both, missy. That was hard for me," he admits.

My cheeks flush even more and my body quivers at the thought of him hard again. I think I finally can admit to myself I'm not just falling off cliffs; I'm falling for Zayn, too.

18

☑ *Parasailing*

☑ *Drive a Jet Ski*

Zayn and I make it to the beach just in time for our parasailing reservation. As soon as we arrive and show our tickets, they get us on the boat as quickly as possible along with another couple on board with us. The two of them, making out and barely coming up for air, don't notice us until they finally take a quick break. The woman moves her sunglasses from resting atop her auburn hair down to her face. She smiles while shouting over the sound of the boat hitting the waves. "Is this the first time for you guys, too?"

"Sure is," Zayn answers.

The woman points to the guy she was locking lips with and says, "He and I just got married this weekend. We're on our honeymoon."

"Aw, that's so sweet," I say. So interesting. Of all the romantic beaches on this earth, who the hell would choose Lake View? Maybe it's becoming a romantic getaway destination with time.

The boat slows down, and the driver asks which couple

would like to go first. The other couple already returned to their intense make-out session; I don't even think they heard him ask. Or noticed the boat stopping, for that matter.

"We'll go," Zayn offers. "That cool with you, Autumn?"

For a second, I'm caught off guard by him calling me Autumn in a not super serious moment. "I'm pretty nervous so . . . let's rip off this Band-Aid before I change my mind."

The instructor hears and gives us a thumbs up, so we head over to him at the back of the boat to get strapped in.

Once we're about to get going, I ask the dreadful question, "What if the rope snaps while we're up there?"

"It won't. And if it does, we'll land in water."

Without a second thought, I grab Zayn's hand. A spark shoots right through me that very minute and I wonder if he feels it too.

"You got this. I promise you, I'm right here with you the whole time. It's going to be okay," he says, placing a small kiss on the back of my hand. My heart does a somersault. "This'll be way less scary than cliff diving, that's for sure."

I nod. "Yeah, you're right. This is fine."

"And you're less likely to lose your top with this one," he says with a wink.

"If it happens this time, I'm crossing skinny-dipping off the list. Even if it's accidental."

"Absolutely not," Zayn says playfully. He sucks his teeth and gives me a little, "Tsk tsk."

The guy starts the boat, and we start to take off. Slowly, we make our way into the air. My grip on Zayn's hand tightens. I'm worried my anxiety is going to rise just like we are in the air right now. Everything beneath us shrinks as it gets farther away.

Once we're completely suspended in the air, everything

feels, well, peaceful. The view of the Atlantic beneath us is surreal. Being up in the air like this reminds me of my first time on a nature hike. The wind blows through the strands of my hair escaping from my ponytail.

"How you doing over there?" Zayn asks.

"Honestly, I'm so calm right now. This is fantastic," I announce. To him. To myself. To the world.

"Yeah, it's awesome," he says.

"Remind me to do this at least once a year, especially when I'm stressed at work. I haven't felt this relaxed in a while," I admit.

He looks at me and smiles. "You should make a list of adventures you want to experience every year. Although, you could simply call yours a YOLO list instead."

I nod, loving the idea. I bite my lower lip from excitement. "I think that might be exactly what Summer intended for me."

"I could see that," he says. "Autumn, I—uh . . ."

"What's up?" I ask, jolted by his use of my first name once again.

"I guess I want to tell you that having you back here at Lake View has been the best thing that's happened to me since Riley. Even with how scared you've been for some of the things we've done, you don't let it stop you. You're courageous. And you make me want to be braver, too."

I tug tighter on his hand before closing my eyes. A tear trickles down my cheek, but I'm not sad; I'm . . . happy.

"Thank you," I say. "Hearing someone call me things like 'courageous' and 'brave' is nice."

He squeezes my hand, and we finish the rest of the ride in comfortable silence, smiling.

When we arrive back on the shore, we spot our friends out on the beach, camped out near our stuff. I can't wait to fill Mason and Natalie in about parasailing. Totally worth it.

"Hey, glad to see you all made it," Zayn says to Mason, Natalie, Ryker, and Taylor. I glance around. No sight of Tori. I breathe out a small sight of relief.

"Hey guys," I say.

"So, how was parasailing?" Taylor asks.

"It was…really nice. Super peaceful, actually. I want to do it every year," I answer honestly.

"It was really great," Zayn says, looking at me.

"I've done it before, but it's been forever. Can't wait to get Taylor out there soon," Ryker says.

"Yes. Speaking of adventures, you guys ready for some jet skis? Our time for rental begins in about fifteen minutes."

"Let's do it!" Ryker says.

We all make our way over to the tent with the jet ski rentals. The woman running the tent is smoking a cigarette and reading a book. When we approach the stand, she pauses from her book to look up at us. "Can I help y'all?" she asks.

"Yes ma'am," Zayn says. "We got three Sea-Doo rentals."

"Three?" Mason interrupts, looking around the group. "There's six of us."

"Well, we can couple up on them, duh." Natalie wraps her arms around Mason's neck. "Share a jet ski with me, please babe? Hope that new boyfriend of yours won't mind," she teases.

"Alright, if I have to," Mason replies, dragging out the last word. "But, if Adam shows up, I'm tossing you in the water, bitch."

Zayn and I exchange a glance instantly. "Your new guy's name is . . . Adam?" I ask.

"Oh, yikes," Mason says before taking his hand to cover

a dramatic gasp. "Yes, sorry. Completely different Adam. One hundred percent. I can't even believe I didn't make that connection." Mason places his hand on his hip.

"Anyway," the woman at the counter says, putting out her cigarette in an empty beer can. "Everyone, come over here and grab a life jacket. It's mandatory you keep them on. Next to those, you'll find a safety card. Read it over before driving. Last thing I need is signatures on this page from everyone for our liability waivers. Any questions?"

None of us say a word as we follow her directions. "Alright kids, here's the keys for three of our Sea-Doos. Take care of those babies and have a good time. I'll be over here if you have any questions. "

"Thank you very much," I say. I turn around to everyone and say, "Life jackets—check. Safety cards—check. Signatures—almost check." I grin at Natalie and Taylor who are the last two to sign.

"We're almost done," Taylor announces.

"Okay, I'll say signatures—check." I watch as Zayn hands a set of keys to Ryker and Mason. Mason shakes his head and points to Natalie, so he hands the set to her instead.

I hold one hand out to Zayn. "Keys, please?"

"Wait, what? You're driving us?" he asks.

I fold my arms across my chest and scoff. "Yeah, it's on my WOLO list. I feel like driving it needs to happen."

"Oooh, she's got ya there, dude," Ryker says like we're in high school again.

Zayn hesitates and blows out a breath. "Okay, fine. Here's the keys. Don't get us killed."

"No promises," I say with a wink. He places them in my hand, and I take off into to the water. I reach the jet ski, push it out further into the water, and hop on. Zayn runs to catch up and yells, "Hey don't take off on that thing without me."

He hops on the back of it and wraps his arms around my waist. My skin prickles at his touch and a shiver shoots down my spine. He hardens against my back. I glance down at what looks like millions of goosebumps forming on my legs. They don't last long as the heat from his skin radiates through me. I might need to hop into the water after this just to cool down.

"You ready?" I ask, tilting my head back toward him. My body pressed against his chest sets a fire in my heart.

"Ready as I'll ever be," he says. I pop the key attached to the keychain bracelet into the designated area before pressing the red start button. We jolt forward.

"Um, how do I get this thing to go?" I yell to Zayn, my hands in the air.

I watch as Zayn takes his hand and guides it to the right handle, showing me the accelerator. "Don't!" he warns, but too late. I squeeze down on it too tight and we bunny hop forward.

The warmth from his hands disappears, and he goes flying off the back of the jet ski. My peripherals show me a flailing Zayn, suspended in midair. By the time I slow down and turn my head to look, I see nothing but choppy water. No sign of Zayn.

Ryker yells out to me, "He's somewhere there. You've got to turn around."

I give a thumbs up before circling back to the location Ryker pointed out.

A few seconds later, I see his head teetering above the water. Natalie shouts, "Zayn, stay where you are! Autumn is coming to you!"

His arms flail above his head.

"I'm coming!" I call out to him, getting closer.

I pull up beside him. "Turn off the engine," he yells to me.

I listen and the Sea-Doo and surrounding water start to calm. I reach my hand out for him. Zayn shakes his head and explains, "I have to get on through the rear. Don't start it up again until I'm on. Okay?"

"Okay," I say breathily.

He holds the back and slowly climbs aboard, fumbling behind me, as he makes his way back onto the seat.

He says, "Alright, I think I'm good now."

"Okay, great." I let out a chuckle. "Uh, sorry about that."

"I should've known that within the first minute, you'd have me booted off this thing." He lets out a large belly laugh. When he catches his breath, he gives our friends a thumbs up. "Okay, everyone. We're back in business."

"Where should we go?" I ask.

Ryker raises his hand and says, "I'll lead the way. You guys follow me."

We all nod in agreement. Ryker takes off, and Natalie follows behind.

"Wait," Zayn says. "Before you start it back up, you know how do it now?"

"Yes, I got a bit more practice while you went for a swim."

He scoffs at my sass. "Oh, real nice. I forgot how badly I wanted to take a leisurely swim today," he says as he slowly places his hands back around my waist. "Heads up that my hands are chilly now."

"Oh, shit." My whole body shivers and I instinctively grab at his hands. Our fingers intertwine and a shock bolts through me. I look back at Zayn, but don't say anything. Instead, we both sit in this moment together. *I wonder if he wants me just as bad as I want him right now.*

"You guys coming?" Mason shouts from the back of his watercraft, ahead of us.

"Yeah," I say, releasing my hands from Zayn even though I don't want to. I grab onto the handles, steering us closer to our friends.

We ride around for a while, laughing as we all watch Ryker scare the shit out of Taylor with his so-called tricks. Zayn shares with me that he and Ryker have only been on jet skis a few times back when he finished EMT training. Despite him and Ryker not growing up with money, he goes on to share that a few of the guys they hung out with did so they had the chance to experience life on the water other than just fishing.

The hour passes quickly. We return to the woman at the rental tent, still smoking and reading her book. Dropping off the keys and life vests, a few of us thank her, but she only throws up a hand and nods.

"I'm literally starving," Mason says dramatically.

"We brought enough food for everyone," I say. "I'm so ready to chill for a bit. It's been a fun day, but I'm wiped."

"Me too," Zayn says, reaching for my hand. I accept and our fingers interlace as we walk along the beach with our friends.

Mason gives me a smirk from the side, and I pretend not to notice.

Once we're back by our stuff, everyone settles in chairs and on beach towels underneath the tent that Ryker brought. I pull out the food—sandwiches, chips, dip, and some fruit kabobs I made.

"Wow, this looks delicious," Taylor comments. "You really took the time to prepare all this."

"Nah, it's no big deal. But you can thank Zayn for his amazing packing skills." I point to Zayn and smile. My smile moves my oversized sunglasses down the bridge of my nose, so I push them back against my face with my finger.

"Thank you, both. Seriously, this looks bomb," Mason says.

"Dig in," I say.

Everyone eats their sandwiches quickly. Zayn gets up and heads to the cooler to grab me a water.

"Can you get out the French Onion dip?" I ask him.

He nods and grabs the dip and a bag of chips next to it before taking his seat next to me on our beach towel.

We share the chips and dip while our friends start chatting and Zayn smiles at me. I smile back, realizing how comfortable I've grown around him since I've been back. I don't know what we are—friends, more than friends—but it feels *right*.

After we've both had a few chips, Zayn stares into the dip container. "Ya know, I never noticed how ruthless you are with the chip dip."

"What?" I ask.

"Yeah, you just stick the chip in anywhere, the sides, the middle, and it makes it all uneven," he explains. "I didn't know you were a chip *caveman*."

I hold my hand in front of my mouth to laugh. "Excuse me," I scoff.

"Excuse you is right," he teases.

"I may like to plan, but you, sir, are such a perfectionist. Even your chip dip has to be evenly spread. That's what isn't normal! I'm the normal one. Right, guys?" I ask, glancing around at everyone. They're all too busy eating their own sandwiches or sunbathing to care about how we eat chips. Taylor and Natalie shrug. Ryker doesn't say a word. Mason uses his hand to shield his eyes to look at us better before he says, "Get a room, you two."

I wave off his comment. *Damn it. Are we that obnoxious*

right now? I find a napkin and wipe the chip grease off my hands. I take another swig of water and think about how I really need to remember that I am not in the mental state to be dating, especially Zayn Mitchell.

"So, what's next on our agenda?" Natalie asks, interrupting my thoughts. "I've got a bit more energy to do another one of your WOLO adventures with you guys."

Zayn and I exchange glances. My lips purse together briefly before I say, "Well, there is one thing we could all do."

Natalie gasps in excitement. "Yes! What is it?"

"Anyone up for burying someone in the sand?" I ask.

"Absolutely not," Taylor says. "It's a huge fear of mine."

Zayn stands to his feet, wiping the sand off him. "Well, you're in luck. It's Autumn's, too."

Taylor looks at me with eyebrows raised above her sunglasses. "So you're gonna do it for the first time?"

"Yeah, I've been doing a lot of firsts this year thanks to my sister, Summer. Long story," I explain. "You guys in or what?"

Everyone's eyes shift around nervously. Mason laughs and says, "Oh, I'm so in."

19

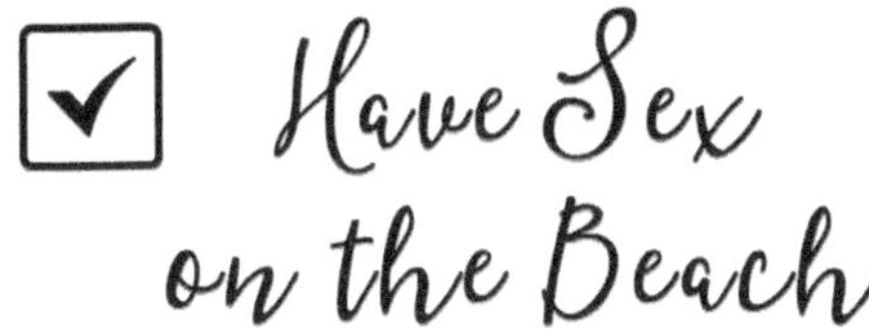

☑ *Have Sex on the Beach*

I've never been more uncomfortable in my entire life. I'd rather have Liam tell me he's remarrying a hundred times than be under the sand like this for a second longer.

Zayn laughs. "You're so uncomfortable under there, aren't you?"

Okay, Mr. Mind reader. "You have no idea."

Mason shouts out, in his best Jean Ralphio from *Parks and Recreation* voice, "This is the woooorst."

All of us laugh, even Ryker, who's buried right alongside me and Mason.

"This is hilarious," Taylor says.

"Yeah, I'd be saying that too if I'd chickened out," Mason quips.

"Sorry about that. But y'all are doing great." Taylor starts to walk away. "Okay guys, let me grab my phone so we can get a picture."

I hear a stranger's voice ask, "Would you like me to take a picture of all you?"

"Yes," Natalie exclaims. "We'd love that! Right, Mace?"

I lift my head as much as I can, watching as Taylor hands over her phone to the girl before sitting right next to our buried trio. Zayn and Natalie join her.

The girl yells out, "Okay, three . . . two . . . one . . . say cheese!"

We all yell 'cheese,' including the three of us in the sand. The girl hands Taylor her phone back and says, "Here you go. I took at least a few."

"Thank you so much," Taylor says, grabbing her phone to scroll through the photos. "You guys, these look awesome."

I shout from the sand, "Yeah, I'd be saying the same thing from up there, too."

Taylor looks down at me. "Girl, I'm so sorry. Maybe next time."

I hear Mason yell out, "Okay, can we get the hell out of here now? I'm starting to suffocate. Claustrophobia is settling in, bitches."

"Yeah, dig us out now, please," Ryker says.

"Hmmm . . . what do you think, guys? Should we get these three out of here?" Zayn teases.

"Nah, let's leave 'em," Natalie says. The three of them must have exchanged some type of wink or private gesture, because they disappear behind us and out of view.

"Ha ha, you guys. Very funny," I say.

They all aren't there, or at least, we still can't see them. Mason yells out, "Yup. This is it. I knew this is how I would die."

"Oh, Mason, stop," I say with a chuckle.

Sure enough, I hear Zayn's laugh in the distance. "Okay, sorry. We had to though, you know?" Zayn says to us as they reappear in front of us.

They all get on their hands and knees and start digging us out.

Once we're free, Mason, Ryker, and I all run into the water to wash the mud and sand off our bodies, splashing each other playfully. I sign and float, letting the ocean waves wash over me as I relax in the water. Despite a few rough waves, the water is so comforting. I look towards the sky and realize how truly happy I am in this moment. I think Summer would be proud. I'm completing the list, I'm being adventurous and stepping out of my comfort zone, and most importantly, I'm realizing that I have some awesome relationships here in my hometown—both new and old.

Dusk settles in on our beach day. Zayn and I tell our friends goodbye and begin walking back to the beach house. On the way to it, he says, "Hey, will Quinton be okay on his own a little longer?"

"He should be fine," I say. "Why do you ask?"

"Because I don't know about you, but I'm already hungry again. Would it be cool with you if we got some take out and ate it back at your place?"

"That sounds perfect," I say, hearing the grumble of my stomach over the sound of the waves crashing against the shore. "I could really go for some pizza, actually. Is Anthony's still around?"

Zayn's eyes light up at the mention of it. "Yes, it is. It's always been one of my favorites," he tells me. "We should definitely go."

WE GRAB a large pepperoni pizza to go and head back to the beach house. By the time we finally make it back, the sun is about to set. I unlock the door and turn on the lights. Zayn gets plates and I grab us some water from the fridge.

I check on Quinton, who is, as usual, sound asleep. Zayn brings over a slice of pizza on a plate for me and sets in on the table. He pulls out my chair and I begin making my way over.

"Let's put some towels down so we don't get the chairs all gross from sweat and sand," Zayn offers.

"Good idea." I pull out fresh towels from the linen closet and set them on each of the chairs. We both sit down and begin scarfing down the slices of pizza. I chug back my glass of water.

"We ate that so quickly," he remarks.

"Yeah, I'm glad you brought up food because I was dying to eat," I say.

"Starting to sound like Mason a bit, huh?" He teases.

"Touché." I smile and then look down at my sunburned body, hoping it will turn into a nice tan. I'm still covered in sand and should really take a shower, but then a better idea comes across my mind. "Hey, this might sound crazy, but do you have one more adventure left in you for the day?"

Zayn perks up and clears his throat.

"Shit, not *that* one," I say. My cheeks flush at his first

thought and I swallow the lump that's formed in my throat. "No, silly. I meant, let's skinny dip."

"Is there a pool nearby?" he asks.

"Nope." I pull down my hair tie, releasing my long hair and allowing it to fall down my back and shoulders. I stand up, grab two more fresh beach towels, and head to the glass sliding door leading out to the patio and the beach. "You comin' or not?" I ask, taking off my beach cover-up dress and tossing it on the couch.

Zayn doesn't say a word but follows me as I lead us outside. With each step, my bare feet sink further into the cool, night sand.

As we get closer to the water, I stop at an open area with damp sand. It's a little more private due to some shrubs and beach grass surrounding it. I double check to make sure no one is around and set the towels down to claim the spot. Adrenaline pumps through every vein in my body. *This is one of the last items remaining on the list*, I remind myself, hoping I'll push through and won't chicken out.

I exhale and yank off my bathing suit top. Even though it's dark out, I can see the whites of Zayn's eyes widen. Without a word, he takes off his bathing suit and stands there naked in front of me. I want nothing more than to peek, but I know he'd notice, so I distract myself with taking my bottoms off. I stand there naked, using my hands to cover my boobs the best I can. "Okay, I'm super anxious."

Zayn looks around. "*Now* is the time you decide to be anxious? You're already standing their buck naked. Let's get in the water."

"Zayn," I say nervously. "I don't know if I can."

He inches closer to me. "Listen, Autumn. A few months ago, you were terrified of life."

I scoff. "I wouldn't go to that extre—"

"No, let me finish," he says sternly. "As I was saying, you were terrified of pretty much everything. You didn't want anything to change, you lived in a bubble, and took no risks. Predictability was how you lived. And now, over the past few months, I've seen you overcome so much. Your fear of change, your anxiety, and your need for predictability. You've taken risks with this list and done things that, let's be honest, you never would've done had Summer not insisted. And . . . you've taken a risk on me. So, say screw anxiety, and get in the damn ocean."

My chest deflates as I exhale through my nostrils. "Okay, fine."

"Say it," he demands.

"Say what?"

"Screw anxiety!"

"Seriously?" I ask about to roll my eyes in the darkness.

"Yes, dammit. Say it," he commands.

I cross my arms fully against my chest. "Fine. Screw anxiety," I say.

"Yell it!"

"Screw anxiety!"

"Scream it like you mean it!"

"Screw anxiety!" I shout at the top of my lungs. If I said it any louder, I'd expect my fists to start beating against my chest like a gorilla.

A giddy scream escapes me as I jet towards the ocean. He follows behind me. I stop short at the water line and look back at him. He catches up a second later and pauses next to me. He grabs ahold of my hand, and we rush into the freezing cold water together.

As soon as we're submerged up to our necks, I paddle frantically to warm myself up, and because I'm suddenly terrified of what creatures could possibly be right beneath us.

"Okay, so if I'm being real. I'm glad we did it, but now I'm freaking out again," I admit to him.

"Come here," he says, pulling my hand in the water and leading my body in front of his. With a final pull, my naked body presses against his. I'm instantly filled with both comfort and desire. I can feel his hand slide down against my butt and my legs naturally wrap around him. His breath slows down as I look into his eyes, visible only from the moonlight. I watch as he looks down. My breasts are pushed up against his chest. I feel him harden. A whimper escapes me. Tingles find their way between my thighs from anticipation.

He clears his throat. "Um, sorry. I can't control the little guy."

I try to stifle it, but I laugh. "Little, huh?"

"Oh, shit," he says. "Hmph. How can I make him sound more badass now? How about I can't control my . . . bald avenger?"

I laugh even harder and so does he.

"Wow, way to kill the mood, Z," I tease.

Zayn clears his throat again, and this time gets serious. "Autumn, I want you more than anyone or anything."

I bite my lower lip in excitement.

Our eyes meet once again before they fall to each other's lips. Memories of our first kiss invade my mind. I close my eyes to wish it away, but it's too late. His mouth presses against mine with intensity. Those pillow lips are once again comforting mine. I turn my head and my tongue finds its way into his mouth. My hands make their way to his soaking wet hair. I run my fingers through it before they make their way down to explore his bare chest. His tongue takes a break, and he softly nibbles on my bottom lip. A moan escapes me. *Am I ready for this? I know it's on the list, but am I ready?*

My desire for him deepens when he looks at me. I have so much to say, but I choose to not to say a word. Instead, I fling my head back as his lips meet my neck. With each kiss, I melt a little more. My legs squirm beneath the surface as I feel him rub against me.

His mouth inches lower down my chest until it reaches my nipple. His lips encompass it and my own part to release a moan. My breath quickens.

I begin to move my hips up and down against him in the water. He stands up completely and lifts us out of the water. The moonlight glistens on our wet bodies. I arch back in the air, and he kisses my stomach. I'm ready to let go and let him in.

Zayn lowers our bodies back into the water. He pulls away again and stares into my eyes. This time he mutters, "I'm sorry."

"What?" His words startle me. "Why the hell are you apologizing?" I ask, wishing he'd stop talking. I'm finally letting go of my anxiety and he's ruining it with an apology.

"Are you sure you want this? I really don't want you to do anything you don't actually want to do." He releases me into the water and grabs my hand. We slowly wade through the water together until we reach the shore.

"Ugh, you know what? No. Stop being sorry," I tell him. "I do want it."

He breathes heavily. "Autumn, let's be real. You don't. We're both caught up in the moment right now. Hell, in a few months once the list is complete, you'll more than likely go back to hating my guts."

"That's not true. I do want you," I admit. My hands guard my chest from the chill that overcomes me. "More than that, I've wanted you for a long time. So much, that I spent my entire adult life, married life included, hoping, praying, and waiting for you, Zayn. Waiting for you to explain why the hell you left me."

He inches closer to me again. "I know. That will forever be the biggest regret of my life."

I cry at his words, feeling like this has been the biggest reason I haven't wanted to give myself to him again. "So is your dad really the only reason you stayed behind?"

He lets out a sigh and rubs his palm against his forehead. "Yes, originally. He made threats to me. He wasn't the guy you see and know today. I thought he was going to try to hurt himself, or worse, someone else."

I watch as his eyes gloss over with tears. "I know it's the stereotypical response, but at the time it really wasn't about you; it was about me. I was only trying to do the right thing by staying to help my dad. Then, I took out all my anger by sleeping with anyone who gave me the time of day." His hands hug the back of his neck. "I was planning to move to NYU the following semester, but then . . . well you know, Riley came into the picture. I tried to make it work with Sam so I could be the father mine never was. I needed to know I tried everything to be a better dad, so I did what I thought I had to do. Clearly, it didn't work out. Which now, I'm glad it didn't. But my regret all along was leaving you."

I wipe my tears. "You were going to come to NYU after that?"

He nods. "I actually took a flight to come surprise you one day. But I saw how happy you were . . . with Liam. So, I knew I had to let you go so you could be happy."

My hands shake and my voice trembles. "You should've told me that. Instead, you ghosted me. I never heard from you again. That was the worst night of my life when you ended things. I had to move on. I needed a new plan."

Zayn wraps his arms around me. He holds my head in his hands, using his thumbs to wipe away my tears. He looks down at me with his bold, brown eyes. "You have always been my plan, Autumn."

I part my lips in a gasp and he lowers his head to meet them once again. I surrender to him in this moment, allowing my hands to explore his body from his neck to his chest and down to where I feel him harden in my hand. My eyes look back up at him.

His eyebrows raise to double check I'm still okay with this. I nod and grab his face again to kiss him. His tongue makes its way back into my mouth and we start to move backwards towards the spot I set our towels down. He pauses for a moment and then grabs one of the towels to lay it down on the sand.

As soon as he does, he comes right back to kissing me again. His hands slip behind me, taking hold of me and lifting me in the air. My legs straddle him while he stands, then lowers himself to the ground, and places me on my back on the towel. My thighs continue to stay wrapped around his waist. He kisses my neck and heads down to my nipples again, carefully caressing each breast before making his way down and tasting every inch of me. My thighs begin to shake from pleasure and then release, and he returns to my eye line with a smile.

"Autumn, you're so sexy. I've never wanted you more."

I whimper in response as he continues kissing me from head to toe. Zayn pauses for a moment. "I uh—shit, I'm so sorry. I don't have a condom on me."

"It's okay. I'm on the pill still actually."

"You sure?"

"Yes, now shut up and get over here." His eyes fill with

lust. I pull him back down towards me. He wraps my legs around his neck and lowers himself down, entering me slowly. My eyes roll back, and he groans with pleasure with every inch.

The moment he's fully inside of me, my back arches and a loud moan escapes me. My anxiety disappears into the darkness. The sounds of the ocean breeze and waves have my back tonight.

20

☑ *Stay Up and Watch the Sunrise*

"It's so breathtakingly beautiful," I say.

I feel Zayn's eyes on me. "I couldn't agree more," he says.

The two of us are still on the beach, our naked bodies pressed up against each other, wrapped up in a beach towel as we watch the sunrise.

He tucks a strand of my hair behind my ear. "It doesn't get any better than this."

"Mhmm." I close my eyes, allowing the warmth of the sunrise to shine down upon us. We've been awake the whole night.

"Ya know, I pull all-nighters for work all the time, this is different. I'm just now getting tired," Zayn tells me.

"You want to head inside and sleep in my bed?" I ask.

He nods. "Yes, I'm definitely ready to crash."

"Same here."

We unwrap ourselves from the towel we're sharing and instead wrap ourselves up in separate ones to head inside.

The feeling of the sand between my toes—and well, a few other places—reminds me that this was one of the best nights of my life.

Once inside, Zayn asks if I want to rinse off together. I wake a bit more at the thought of a shower with him, so I agree. *I mean, we did just have sex on the beach, so YOLO.*

The moment we step inside the shower, we're right

back to kissing and making love again before finally washing off.

I gently take my lathered loofah to his body, slowly washing away the sand. We trade off and he lathers me in return. It feels like this may be the most intimate thing I've ever done. Before long, I find myself turning, breasts pressed up against the glass of the shower door, with him inside of me for a second time.

THE SOUND of the alarm on my phone wakes me, so I roll over to turn it off on my nightstand. I look next to me to find Zayn. *He is so cute, even when he's asleep.* I stand up and locate my slippers before heading to the bathroom to freshen up for the day.

When I'm done, I check to see if he's awake yet. I sit on the edge of the bed debating whether I should wake him.

I decide against it—the man needs rest on his day off— so I head to the kitchen to make some coffee. As I'm about to start up the coffee maker, Zayn enters the kitchen wearing nothing but his boxers. I inhale as my mind starts to wander about the amazing night we had.

"Good morning, sunshine," he says wiping his eyes.

"Morning," I say. "Coffee?"

"Yes, but not here. Let's go out."

I'm so tired, but it would be nice to get some fresh air and a fancier coffee. I swear iced coffee is one of my love languages.

"Hmm, okay. Want to grab a Starbucks?" I ask.

He gets closer to me, and I can't help but stare at his

defined abs. *Liam was always in shape, but this man looks like he works out several times a day. Maybe firefighters do?*

"Autumn, hello?" he says interrupting my thoughts.

My eyes widen and I blink myself into focus. "Sorry. What's up?"

He chuckles. "I asked if you wanted to go to Eats & Sweets? Like old times." I watch as he runs his fingers through his hair and looks down at the ground.

"Um," I pause. We have so many memories together at Eats & Sweets from our high school days. Sure, we'd still go to Starbucks occasionally, but that place was so special. Sometimes we would just hang out there after school, eating a variety of bizarre-combination donuts like peanut butter and bacon donut or a cheeseburger donut. The place itself though always reminded me of Central Perk from the show *Friends*, with its odd couches and inviting atmosphere.

"Am I losing ya again today, Autumn?" Zayn asks.

"Shit. Sorry about that. Yeah, that sounds great. I'll go get ready," I say turning back towards my bedroom. "We're walking, right?"

"Yeah, let's enjoy the sunshine. Maybe it'll wake us up a bit more, too."

I nod before ducking into the bedroom to get dressed.

ZAYN OPENS the door to Eats & Sweets and a rush of memories flood my mind. I'm brought back to the first time we ever came here. Zayn wrote a cheesy napkin note —that I loved—that said, *I'll love you forever, donut you worry.* I made fun of him for it, of course, but then it started this trend of writing little notes to each other on their unique Eats & Sweets napkins.

We get in line, and I glance over at the donut options. "Ooh, Zayn, look! Heart-shaped ones," I say as though I'm a little kid. I won't lie; donuts are one of my favorite treats. When it's our turn to order, Zayn orders us two coffees, one iced with caramel and one black as well as two heart donuts.

"You remembered my coffee order here?" I ask, feeling a bit shocked.

He shrugs. "Nah, lucky guess."

I chuckle. "What if I, oh I don't know, changed up my order since my high school days?"

He hands the barista his card and his lips form a smirk. "Wait, did you?"

"Nope," I answer.

"I had a feeling," he teases. The barista's eyes shift back and forth between us, and she smiles before handing us our order.

Thanking her briefly, I find a comfy open chair near a window for us to sit. We scoot next to each other, and there in front of us are the napkins. I watch Zayn as he searches his pants pocket for something.

"You got a pen?" he asks me.

I shake my head.

"I'll go ask the barista to borrow one," he says, getting up from the chair. When he's up at the counter, I notice someone staring at me from the corner of my eye. Turning my head just slightly so that I don't rudely glare back, I see a head of curly, blonde hair. My mind starts to race. I finally get the guts to do a full glance to see if my suspicions are correct. Yup. It's Tori.

This girl pops up everywhere. She smiles at me, and I offer an awkward wave right as Zayn returns with a pen.

He's so focused on the napkin that he doesn't even notice Tori at the table next to us.

His phone starts to ring.

"Wow, that's quite the ringtone," I comment as it beeps obnoxiously, disturbing the coffee shop peace.

"Shit," he says pulling it out from his pocket. "That's the ring from the station. They must be calling me in." Answering with a quick "hello," he walks over to a quiet spot in the cafe. I watch as he pinches the area between his eyes and slowly rubs his eyebrows. One good thing about teaching is at least I'm not on call like this—how stressful. Although, receiving a nastygram email or phone call (made that mistake my first year) from a parent at nine o'clock on a Tuesday night isn't so fun either. I blow out a sigh, thinking of how far I've come when it comes to setting boundaries. Yet, still so much more to go.

Zayn rushes over to me. "Hey, I'm so sorry but I have to go."

"It's okay, Z. I understand," I say and mean it. "I'll be fine. I could use a bit of rest anyway. Hope everything is alright at the station."

"Thanks, me too," he says grabbing the napkin he was starting to write on before the call. "I'm not forgetting this, though." He stuffs it into his pocket.

I smile. "Can't wait to read your cheesy note." I put his donut in the bag and hand it to him along with his coffee. "To go," I say.

"Yup, guess so. Thanks," he says before leaning down and giving me a kiss. I'm caught off guard, but I kiss him back. He bites my lower lip and I let out a small moan. He pulls away. "Oof, this isn't how I envisioned the rest of our day together."

"Me neither, but I get it."

"You're the best. Okay, gotta run. See ya soon," he says and makes his way out the door.

I take a sip of my iced coffee and lean back in the comfy chair. *I wish I brought a book or my phone.* Leaning forward, I grab the heart-shaped donut and take a bite. Pure sugar, but I love the jolt it gives me. Before I take a second bite, Tori takes a seat in front of me.

"Hey, it's Autumn, right?"

"Um, hi," I manage to say. "Yes. Tori?"

She nods. "Yup."

Her blue eyes pierce through mine. "Is there anything I can help you with?"

Tori shakes her head and lets out a laugh. "Oh, no. Nothing really. I guess I'm just a bit curious . . . are you and Zayn officially together?"

Damn, what is with her? Why is this any of her business? Does she want him back?

I hesitate before giving her a, "Well, sort of."

She nods. "Mhmm." she takes a sip of her coffee and places it down on the table with the napkins. "I had a feeling that was the case."

I watch as she scoots her chair closer to the table, as if leaning in to let me in on a secret.

"Excuse me?" I ask.

"So, here's the thing. Not sure if you know this, but Zayn and I were together a few years back. We hooked up one night and next thing you know, we were talking nonstop and having all sorts of fun together . . ." She pauses to take another sip of coffee. Jealousy rages through my veins and seeps out of every pore as I start breaking into a sweat. I grab a napkin off the table between us and dab slightly at my forehead and cheeks.

"Sorry, I'm a bit hot, I guess," I tell her.

"Even with iced coffee?" she inquires.

I scoff. "I guess so. Anyway, you and Zayn had fun together, got it." I'm not usually this rude, but I don't know how to get out of this sticky situation.

"Honey, please. I am not the bad guy here. But yeah, you get the gist. For the months we were together, we made plans, like to move in together or whatever. Instead, the man tells me we're over. That we had been over for some time. And poof—just like that, it's as if we were nothing."

"I—wait, when did this happen?" I ask.

"About four years ago. I know, I sound pathetic. But us girls have to look out for each other, ya know?" Tori flashes me a smile.

I nod. "Yeah, definitely. I appreciate that. And I am so sorry he did that to you."

"Eh, it's whatever now. Water under the bridge. Our first night together was so amazing. I'll never forget how I thought my life had changed for the better and that I'd finally found 'the one' . . . sounds silly, I know."

I cough. "Not silly. I know the feeling myself."

"I bet. I'm not trying to be negative. And to be honest with you, I've come to appreciate what we had even if he did end it like that. Such a shame, isn't it? The good-looking guys are always douchebags." Tori takes another sip of her coffee before standing. "Look, Autumn, I know it can be hard to hear this, but just be careful is all. Good luck."

"Thanks, Tori. I will be."

"Bye," she says flashing me a quick wave.

"Bye." I blow out a sigh. *Well, that was . . . a lot. So, Zayn ghosted her, too. Do I honestly know if he wants to commit?* My mind flashes back to his mention of their relationship being "nothing," and that he shouldn't have let it go on for as long as it did. Maybe that's what's happening to us now.

21

Zayn

*N*o response. I need to go see her. It's weird I haven't heard from her. She hasn't returned my calls in almost two days. Two whole days since our amazing night and morning we shared together. And now, nothing. Crickets.

I pop on my favorite Under Armor hoodie and the mixture of Autumn's perfume and coconut shampoo enters my nostrils. Instantly, her scent takes me back to the days when I first asked her out.

TWELVE YEARS AGO

I can't believe I scored the winning touchdown tonight! I feel so bold, so good. I walk toward the stands and several girls instantly approach me. I start to debate who will be the lucky girl for me tonight. Scanning the bleachers, my eyes meet hers. There's the girl I've always wanted, laughing with a few of her friends.

Autumn Parker.

She's wearing jeans and a Lake View High hoodie, and she's easily the most beautiful girl here tonight. Seeing her long, brown hair in those two braids flow down her sweatshirt is about to kill me. Every time I see her, my whole body freezes. Her smile automatically makes me smile too. I'd been with lots of girls, but no one can match this feeling I have when I'm around her.

Not to brag, but approaching girls typically comes easy for me. In fact, they often come up to me first, which I know has a lot to do with being a football player. I don't really get why. It's just a sport, and right now, I'm so sweaty and probably smell like wet towels and onions. But there's at least a dozen girls flocked around me.

I smile, nodding politely as I wade through the small sea of them. As I get closer to Autumn and her friends, I realize I don't know what to say to her.

I look down and notice the dirt under the stands beginning to show through what used to be grass. I focus on my surroundings instead. When my feet finally manage to take me to her, all I'm able to muster is a simple "hi."

She looks right at me. Concern washes over her, yet she still throws me the most magnificent smile as she replies with "hi" back. Nerves flutter in my stomach. I clear my throat, hoping to rid the lump that's formed in it.

Her friends nod in quick approval as they walk away. "I was . . . umm, well. I was wondering," I stumble to get the words out. I clear my throat again. She probably thinks I'm some sort of nut job. "Would you like to . . . go with me?"

Her eyebrow raises in confusion. "Go where?"

Really, Zayn? She's going to think you're a loser. "Uhh . . . sorry, I meant, go out with me." I take a big deep breath before asking, "Would you like to go out with me sometime? Maybe this weekend?"

Autumn blinks a few times before saying, "No, thank you."

"I'd love to pick you up and take you to this new restaur— wait. I'm sorry. Did you say, 'No thank you' to me?" Wow, do I sound like a douchebag.

She drops her phone in her bag and grabs out her keys. "Yes, that's what I said."

"Oh." Embarrassed, I begin to walk away.

Wait, I've come this far with courage, so I feel like I deserve to know why not. Both my feet turn to face her again. I look at her daringly and ask, "Can I at least know why not?"

She stands up, fumbling with her keys. I continue to watch Autumn as she tucks a strand of hair behind her ear and asks me in rebuttal, "Can I know why?"

I'm stunned by her boldness.

She continues, "Tell me why, Mr. Zayn Mitchell, quarterback of the football team, who's known me for years and has barely ever made real eye contact with me, suddenly wants to go out with me?"

I contemplate how best to answer. "Listen, Autumn, I can give you lines about how gorgeous you are like I usually do with the other girls. And yes, believe me, you're one of the most gorgeous girls I've ever laid eyes on. But the truth is . . ." I pause for a moment, staring down at my cleats. It's now or never Zayn, just tell her how you feel. "The truth is that I feel some type of connection with you. I have for years, but I never thought a girl like you would ever take a chance on a guy like me. But then, seeing you here tonight, I figured it's now or never. I just know you'd be good for me. And as bold as it may be for me to assume, I think I could be good for you, too."

As soon as I finish, I search her eyes, trying to make out what she is thinking. I certainly can't read her as easily as I can most girls. Hell, I am not sure I can read her at all. Why is she so different?

"Okay," she replies.

My left eyebrow raises and my head cocks in uncertainty. "Okay? Is that a yes, then?" I ask.

"Yes." Her eyes squint a bit. "But under one condition."

My face softens as I flash her a reassuring smile. I try to mentally prepare myself for whatever her condition might be. "All right, Miss Parker, name your price."

"If this turns out to be some silly joke, and you stand me up

or something, then I will never, EVER speak to you again. Don't mistake my kindness as weakness. Got it?"

I scoff. She thinks this is a joke! Am I that much of an asshole that she doesn't even believe that I really want to go out with her?

"It's not a joke, I promise," I tell her, fighting back the temptation to stick my pinky finger out like a twelve-year-old girl. I continue, "Look, I know I've never given you the chance to get to know me, but I promise you that I'm not the guy that everyone else seems to think I am. That's just who they want me to be, not who I actually am." At this point, I don't think I'm even trying to convince her as much as I am myself. It feels so good to let some of these pent-up feelings out. I release a loud sigh before asking, "So, I'll pick you up at eight p.m. this Friday?"

"Make it six p.m. and you got yourself a deal." Her lips form a smile.

"You're an early bird, huh?" I tease.

She flashes me a big smile as she says, "Definitely. Don't you know . . . the early bird gets the worm?"

That day I decided I wanted to be the earliest bird there ever was.

When I reach the beach house, I ring the doorbell, hoping she'll answer.

The door opens slightly and her face peeks through. "What are you doing here?"

"I—uh, well I'm wondering why you haven't answered any of my calls. What's going on?"

She motions for me to come in. "Zayn," she says. I hear the seriousness in her voice, and I immediately sense that something is off. Her green eyes stare into mine. "I can't do this anymore."

Her words cut like a knife to my heart. "Autumn, please tell me what's going on." My voice cracks a bit. "Please."

"You won't get it, Zayn. I'm sorry we can't all have it so

easy and just go run off into the sunset." My heart sinks at my own words from the past used against me.

"Please don't do this. Can you at least tell me what happened? I'm so confused."

Her arms cross against her chest. "This—you and me—I never should've allowed to happen, that's all. We can be *friends*, just like you wanted, remember?"

"You know that's not what I meant. Things have changed between us . . . or so I thought. I don't understand," I say.

"It's fine, Zayn. It's just I realized I can't do this anymore." I watch as she quickly wipes away a tear from her eye. *Why is she doing this?*

I decide to ask her the same question she asked me years ago. "So, we're just over, then?"

Autumn nods her head in response. She walks to the door and holds it open with her foot while her hands pointedly show me the way out.

I hang my head and make my way to the door. I stuff my hand in my pocket to retrieve the note I wrote her at Eats & Sweets and place it in her hand. "Here, please read it," I beg.

"Fine," she says tossing it on her front entryway table before closing the door behind me. I stand there with my phone in my hand and lean my head against the door. *What the fuck just happened?*

I CAN'T BELIEVE it's already Christmas Eve. I haven't been this down around Christmas since the first one when my dad started taking too many pills and drinking his life away. I remember waking up that Christmas morning to find no presents under the tree—the tree I put up with Ryker's help. When I asked my dad where the presents were, he tried to convince me Christmas was next week. A week later, still no gifts.

I still can't believe he's staying at my place right now. He swears he's been sober for almost a year, and I think this time it's for real. He's honestly been great with Riley, too.

"Dad, can we do that many lights on our house next year?" Riley asks me, interrupting my thought. We're watching *National Lampoon's Christmas Vacation*, one of my all-time favorites.

"I don't know about that, bug. Look at all the trouble he's going through with that many."

She laughs. I flash her a big smile. It's so good to have Riley home with me this week for her winter break. I've missed out on spending the past two Christmases with her since I was scheduled to work, but it's finally worked out this year that I'm off on both Christmas Eve and Day. We spent last night decorating the tree with my dad, and I have to admit, it does feel like things are finally coming together. Except I still haven't heard from or seen Autumn since our breakup. If you can even call it that.

The front door swings open and dad enters carrying a few grocery bags.

"Oh dad, let me help you bring some stuff in," I offer.

My dad gives me a smirk and says, "It ain't much, but thanks. You might want to grab the heavier ones I left out in the car."

Grabbing two bags from him, I ask, "Did you get stuff for dinner?"

"Nope, didn't have to. We've got dinner plans elsewhere."

"We do? Where?" Riley asks right as I'm about to.

"At your teacher's house."

A lump rises in my throat. "Wait, what?" I ask.

Dad nods. "Her mother was at the supermarket and invited us all over for Christmas Eve dinner. Cathy was always such a peach. I couldn't help but say yes. Hope that's alright with you two." He places the bags he's holding onto the kitchen counter.

Riley looks at me with beaming eyes. "Dad, did you hear that? We're having dinner with Ms. Parker!"

"Yeah, that'll be great, but I think it's best we stay in tonight," I say, hoping to hide my hesitation. *Does Autumn know we're coming? How do I get out of this?*

"Dad, no! I want to go," Riley says giving me puppy dog eyes. "Please?"

"Fine." I can never say no to her when she says please.

"Cathy said six o'clock. I bought a couple bottles of wine." He throws his hands up in the air. "Not for me, of course, but for the hosts. Oh, and some cheese dip. Looked pretty good."

The excitement from the two of them make me feel more at ease. I still fear Autumn's going to be not so thrilled that I'm showing up to her family's Christmas Eve dinner. I haven't told my dad, or well . . . anyone about our split. Shit. I guess now there's nothing more to do but show up and hope that my *friend* is excited to see me.

"Sounds great," I say as I'm about to walk out the door. "I'll go grab the rest of the groceries and then we can start getting ready."

"Yay!" Riley exclaims, jumping up off the couch. "I can't wait to go see my favorite teacher! This is gonna be the best Christmas ever!"

I smile at Riley before heading out the door. "I sure hope so," I whisper to myself.

AFTER ABOUT EIGHTEEN OUTFIT CHANGES—FROM both me and Riley—we finally arrive at the Parker's residence. I've been to their beach house so many times now, but never to their family house away from the shore.

Excited, Riley is the first one up the front porch steps. She makes her way to the door and turns to me to see if she can knock on the door, and I give her a nod for the go-ahead. A small dog begins to bark and Autumn's dad, Dan, answers the door.

"Hey, there. You guys made it. We're so happy to have you. Come on in," he says, waving us all inside their cozy home.

I walk in and am instantly hit with the aroma of meat roasting in the oven along with a hint of gingerbread. It smells amazing and takes me back to the times we spent at my grandma's house for Christmas. I look around at all the red, gold, and green garlands and lights. Small figurines of Santa and Mrs. Clause along with a sled and reindeer sit near the door, greeting guests as they enter. Garland is strung across every banister in the house, and little snowmen and angels stand about on the tables and shelves. I'm glad I decided to wear the Christmas sweater Riley gave me a few years ago.

Dan leads us through the foyer and into the living room. There isn't a TV on, but I hear Christmas music. I look down and spot a CD player switched on. *I can't believe she gave me shit about the one in my truck. I didn't think portable ones still existed, though.*

Cathy enters the room to greet us. She's so warm and friendly, with bright green eyes that match Autumn's.

"Welcome, welcome. So glad y'all could make it. Please make yourselves at home."

"Thanks for the invite," my dad says.

"Glad I ran into ya, Rick. It's been years. And there's our sweet Riley and Zayn. I know Autumn will be so pleasantly surprised to see you both."

I swallow. *She doesn't know I'm here. This isn't good.* "We brought a few things," I say holding up the bag and wine.

"Oh wonderful, I'll go pop these in the kitchen. Dinner is ready, so go on and make your way into the dining room. I'll be right there," Cathy says.

Dan leads the way as I follow behind Riley and my dad towards their dining room—yet another ornately decorated room filled with holiday spirit. My father goes to take a seat at the other end of the table, and as soon as he clears the view, I see Autumn. Her beauty lights up the room even more. I can't help but notice her bright red dress with puffy sleeves—a favorite type of hers to wear. Some of her hair is tossed in a little bun that rests right on top of her head. She looks so cute and sexy all at the same time. My eyes instinctively shift towards her lips. I can't help but notice the extra shine on them from her lip gloss. I gnaw on my lower lip to refrain myself from leaping across the table to her. Especially after the last time we were together. Well, before she ended things.

Riley runs over to her and gives her a big hug before taking a seat next to her. When she notices me, her jaw drops. "Zayn?"

I wave. "Hey, Autumn."

Her dad notices, "Y'all over here acting like strangers outta nowhere."

"Oh no, we're still good friends," she says. There's that damn word again—friends. "Just haven't seen each other in a while with our busy schedules."

My thoughts are interrupted when she gestures for me to take a seat. I look around, realizing I'm the only one not yet sitting. Hopefully they all didn't notice me gawking at Autumn. I take my seat across from her and Riley, cushioned between Dan and my dad.

Autumn hops up from her seat and says, "Oops, looks like we're missing the rolls and mashed potatoes. Riley, want to help me grab those?"

She agrees instantly and goes into the kitchen to help Autumn. I take a few sips of water from the table and a few moments later, Riley and Autumn return with the side items. Autumn looks around at the table and says, "Oh, looks like I forgot the wine, too. Sorry guys, I'll be right back."

Riley already sat down, so I offer, "Here, I'll help you grab it. I don't mind." I want to have at least one second alone with her to see where we really stand.

Autumn forces a smile and I follow her into the kitchen. We head straight for the wine on the counter without exchanging a word. She quickly grabs the bottles, and then points to a cabinet and asks me if I can grab two extra wine glasses.

"Sure thing," I tell her. I clear my throat and add, "Sorry if you didn't realize we were showing up. Apparently, Cathy saw my dad at the store and invited us."

"It's no big deal," she says, standing in the door frame between the kitchen and dining room, waiting for me to grab the glasses. "Wait, will your dad be drinking?" she asks.

I shake my head and open the cabinet door, pulling only one wine glass down from the shelf. As I meet her in the door frame, I notice her eyes are closed. Standing next to her, I hear her whispering a checklist of all the food items to herself. She opens her eyes and looks directly in mine. "Okay," she says taking a deep breath. "I think we officially got everything."

"You sure we don't need five more trips?" I tease.

Holding the two bottles of wine, she elbows me playfully in the arm. I chuckle and feel a wave of comfort. *Maybe things aren't so different.* Her eyes shift up above our heads and widen. I look up to see what's caught her attention and realize it's a mistletoe. *Shit.*

"Don't even think about it," she says.

"I . . . wasn't. I'm not," I respond in an almost whisper, both of us knowing I'm lying through my teeth right now. "Autumn, I—can we please talk?"

Her dad yells from the dining room, "You guys coming or what?"

It's too late. Her face turns red before she shouts frantically, "Uh, yeah, we're coming!"

I set the glass down in front of me and Autumn fills it right away. She walks back around to the opposite side of the table where her seat is, setting the bottles down. I watch as she glances over the table one final time and smiles. *God, she is so cute, even when she's stressing over the small stuff.*

Cathy interrupts my thoughts to announce, "Well, thank you all so much for being here tonight on Christmas Eve. Before we dive in, would anyone like to say grace?"

I'm not very religious, but a part of me feels like Cathy is wanting, or maybe even expecting me to volunteer to say it. Dan clears his throat. *Hey, what have I got to lose?*

"I'd be happy to," I answer. I watch Cathy shoot Autumn a look, but I don't have time to investigate that one further.

We all grab hands and bow our heads. I clear my throat, and begin, "Dear Lord, we thank you for this lovely meal we're about to eat. And we thank you for this time together with loved ones who have been apart for so long. Please bless this food and our bodies. We are so excited to have this meal together," I cringe as the words awkwardly fall out my mouth. *I need to end this, like yesterday.* "Thank you again for all you do. In your precious name, Amen."

"Amen," everyone else says in unison.

Riley looks directly at me from across the table and asks, "Dad, how come we don't pray before we eat our meals?"

My face reddens. *Have kids, they say.* "Umm, I don't know, to be honest with ya, bug." My eyes shift towards my father whose eyes soften with a bit of regret. I wave a hand in his direction to show him subtly it's no big deal.

"Oh, okay. Well, can we eat now?" Riley asks.

"We can do that," I say with a smile. Hoping to change the topic, I ask, "So, Dan and Cathy, how have you both been doing?"

They exchange a cute glance with one another before they say in unison, "We're doing great." My eyes find Autumn and her lips part to release a small chuckle. I look back at her parents and can't help but think how amazing it'd be to find a love like theirs. I've always held onto the idea that Autumn and I were meant to be, but maybe I'm wrong. Maybe we're just meant to be friends. *Would I be okay with that?*

"So, Autumn tells us you two have had a lot of adventures together lately, hm?" Cathy asks as she plops a serving of mashed potatoes onto her plate. I exhale. *This is going to be a lot more awkward than I imagined.*

"We have, indeed," I say. Autumn looks at me with a sparkle in her eye, and my face heats up even more. "Autumn here is a brave one."

"Autumn, brave?" her dad asks. Hairs stand up on the back of my neck as if they're preparing for battle.

"She sure is," I say defending her.

"Well, I've gotten a lot of help from Zayn," she says.

"What's the story behind all these random adventures?" My dad asks.

Autumn and I exchange glances. She takes a sip of her wine and says, "Zayn's been helping me with this sort of bucket list that my sister and I created."

"Oh, very cool. Makes sense why y'all went cliff diving off Sunrise Rock then."

"You went cliff diving?" Cathy and Riley ask in unison.

Autumn chuckles. "That's right. I did. In fact, I've had a lot of adventures. The only one missing is getting a tattoo."

"That's so cool," Riley exclaims.

"Ah, tattoos. Never was a fan of 'em myself. You have any tattoos, Rick?" Dan asks my dad.

"I've got a couple from back before Zayn here was even born. What about you, Cathy?" I watch as Dan and Cathy shake their heads at the same time.

Cathy takes a sip of wine and says, "Dan's not a fan, but I'm trying to convince him to get one with me for our thirtieth wedding anniversary. Coming up next year already."

My eyebrows raise. "Oh, wow . . . thirty years? That's impressive."

"Sure is," my dad says. "I'm still waiting on this one to get married." He points to me.

All my blood rushes to my face, and I slowly turn my head, trying to subtly give him a death glare. I set my fork down on my plate and brush my hair back nervously.

Cathy changes the subject. "Well, we can't believe we're going to have a twenty-nine-year-old over here this week."

"December twenty-ninth, right?" I ask, even though I've never forgotten.

"Mhmm," Autumn says.

My dad reaches across the table, spooning more corn

casserole onto his plate. "Alright, son, you best get something nice for your girlfriend then."

I damn near choke on a spear of asparagus. I grab my wine glass and before I can even take a sip, Autumn interjects, "We're actually just friends." The words pierce through me.

She glares at me. My eyes widen from nearly choking, but I finish off the last little bit of my wine. I really need a chance to talk with her more.

"Uh, more wine anyone?" Dan asks as he grabs an unopened bottle off the table. *Dan the Man to the rescue.*

"Yes, please," Autumn and I answer in unison holding up our glasses.

22

☑ Get a Tattoo

"**W**ell, today's the big day," I tell Quinton while holding him. "Definitely hope it's a day to get my mind off of Zayn for once."

"Trust us, it will. We're here!" Natalie announces as she and Mason let themselves in.

I turn and set Quinton back in his home. "Talk to you soon, buddy," I whisper to him before walking into the kitchen to wash my hands. "Hey, guys! Thanks for coming over!"

"We wouldn't miss it for the world. Happy birthday," Mason says coming over to give me a hug. Natalie follows him. The three of us do a group hug for a moment before Mason says, "Love you both so much. Let's make this Autumn's best day ever!"

The two of them send me out onto the patio with an iced coffee from Eats & Sweets. The gesture is sweet and appreciated, but if they knew it reminded me of Zayn, they probably would have brought me Starbucks today instead.

They decorate the house while I sip my coffee and people-watch on the beach. After about ten minutes, they call me inside. Everything is hedgehog themed. I walk around gasping at all the cuteness, when I realize they've put a tiny birthday hat on Quinton, too. It's adorable! They have really outdone themselves. "You guys!" I say, holding my hand to my mouth. A tear makes its way down my cheek. "This is the absolute sweetest. Thank you so much!"

"You are more than welcome, babe," Natalie says,

making some sangria in the kitchen. The doorbell rings so I head over. It's my parents.

"Happy birthday to our sweet little angel," my mom says coming in for a hug. From behind her my dad says, "Happy birthday, Autumn. We love you so much."

"Thank you both. Wait til you see the place. Natalie and Mason really outdid themselves," I tell them.

"You would've done the same for us," Natalie shouts out from the kitchen.

As soon as we all begin heading to the living room, the doorbell rings again. It's some people from work. "Hey guys," I say. "Come on in."

"Happy birthday!"

As soon as they're in, a few others arrive. I take a moment to think to myself how nice it is to be surrounded by family and friends I love. *This is exactly what I needed today.*

I stand at the door, welcoming more people in as they wish me a happy birthday and give hugs. I'm about to shut the door when I notice someone else coming up the driveway. My stomach drops when I see who it is.

Liam.

"Happy birthday, Autumn," he says. "Don't worry, I come in peace."

"Thanks, but what the hell are you doing here? Don't you have a wedding to plan?" I quip.

Liam clears his throat and loosens his tie a bit. "Yup, I deserve that." He peeks inside for a moment. "I know you've got a party going on, but if I could just chat with you for a little, it'd really mean a lot to me. I completely respect if your answer is no, though."

Ugh, do I really want to let this jerk inside right now? I debate it for a moment. "Autumn, come over here really quickly," my mom shouts from the living room.

"Okay, fine," I tell Liam. "You get five minutes. I'll meet you back outside here in a minute. Let me go see what my mom needs and tell the guests I'll be in a quick chat. Sound good?"

"That'd be great," he replies. "I'll wait right here."

I shut the door and make my way into the living room.

"Who's been at the door?" Mom asks. "Is it Zayn? It's weird he isn't here yet."

I release a loud sigh. "No, it's Liam. He says he wants to talk for a few minutes. Probably inviting me to his next wedding already." I roll my eyes and cross my arms. "I told him I'd give him five minutes."

"Oh, dear. You can tell him no if you'd prefer. He has no business dropping you like a potato and then showing up on your birthday. Especially since he's engaged to someone else." My mom folds her arms across her chest, and I can tell she's getting into full-blown mama bear mode.

I nod my head and lower my arms to my sides. "It's whatever at this point, Mom. Don't worry, I can handle it. Be right back."

By the time I get back to the door, I push Liam back outside so we can chat in the front with some privacy. It also assures he'll get the message he is not invited inside and needs to leave right after our chat. When I step onto the porch, I notice he's holding a gift in his hands. My eyebrows raise. "You got me a birthday present?" I ask.

He clears his throat. "Well, this is awkward. No, it's actually not from me. Some guy came by and asked me to bring this in and give to you. Dark hair. Brown eyes."

"Oh," I say, taking the gift bag and clutching it next to me.

"You alright?" Liam asks me.

I blink the thoughts of Zayn away and answer, "Yeah,

fine. Let's sit on the bench." I glance at my watch. "You've got five minutes. Go."

He takes a seat and adjusts his coat. *Why the hell is he even wearing a suit and jacket right now?* The thought makes me realize I don't miss this lifestyle of constantly trying to keep up with the Joneses.

"First, I want to start by apologizing. We ended so quickly, and it wasn't right how I treated you. I could've, err—should've, done better. You didn't deserve that. Hell, I didn't deserve you." He clears his throat. "You and I were so compatible, we didn't take silly risks, we planned it all out. The predictability was so nice."

My left eyebrow raises in suspicion.

"But now I'm with Leah. And nothing is predictable. She barely even wants to plan the wedding—she wants to 'play it by ear' and 'wing it.' It's stressing me out and making me think maybe I've made a huge mistake."

I bite my tongue. It's taking everything inside of me to refrain from saying something rude and laughing in his face for suggesting he needs my blessing for him to be with some other woman. But something holds me back. I notice the worry, sadness, and fear in his eyes. That familiar fear I know so well. The fear of change.

"Liam, you and I may have been more compatible on paper, but in reality, we were just going through the motions. Adhering to whatever societal expectations we thought we were supposed to do. And honestly, as much as I hated the timing of it all since you left me right when my own sister was dying, the changes I was forced to make . . . that was the fuel I needed to change. You and I lived a surface level life. The unpredictability of life—reality—is the depth you need in order to grow."

Liam interrupts, "But, Autumn, that's not true. You and I were so successful. Sure, you were just a teacher, but look at what I did. The money I was making for us, the nice things we had, the traveling we got to do."

I cringe at the words *just a teacher*. Right now, I have to choose my battles, and there's a bigger battle to fight here. "Liam," I say, taking his hands in mine. "Those are all just *things*. Success doesn't always equate to more money. It certainly doesn't equate to working so often that you never see your family. Success is accomplishing your goals and is different for everyone. That's where we messed up. We let other people define our success and then couldn't understand why we weren't happy."

"Wow, Autumn. You really have changed," he says, taking back his hands and slouching on the bench. "So, you think I should take the risk with Leah? Be okay without a definite plan?"

I close my eyes for a moment before I tell him, "One thing I've learned is we can try to plan all we want, but most of the time, life doesn't go according to the plan. And, who cares if you aren't perfectly compatible on paper? If your hearts are, that's all that matters." I open my eyes and grab his hand before I continue, "Summer knew the secret to life. It's meant to be messy, and most importantly, it's meant to be lived. I think you should trust your heart, Liam. Love always finds a way."

I see a tear stream down his cheek. "You're right. I feel such relief when I don't have to second-guess everything with a risk analysis or plan out my next five, ten, fifteen years. Seems silly when you put it in that perspective." He stands to his feet, buttoning his jacket. "Thank you, Autumn. You've always been selfless, but now you've given me a gift on your birthday. I appreciate it."

"Yeah, yeah, no problem," I say, checking my watch. "Well, I better get back inside. Don't want to keep everyone waiting on me. Bye, Liam."

I watch him walk to his BMW. I head back inside and step towards the party, but then I see the note I left on my entryway table that Zayn gave me before I kicked him out the other day—the napkin he took from Eats & Sweets. I stare at his handwriting on it.

My dear Autumn,
In this one life we get to live, I will love you for all of mine.
Forever yours,
Zayn

I take the note in my palm and head back out the door. I sneak around in the garage to take a moment to catch my breath. Opening the side door, I peek my head in first, ensuring it's empty. I walk in and pull the thread to turn the light bulb on. Taking a seat on a storage container, I hold the napkin up to my heart. *This feels so unfair. Is Tori right? Is he just going to break my heart again?* A part of me wants to run away from it all. Maybe head back to Connecticut or California or something and start all over again.

But then it hits me. I can't even believe I'm thinking this, but . . . my hometown is home now. I don't miss the hustle and bustle of the city. I don't miss the constant chase to always get the next best thing. And I don't miss living a life where I was completely unhappy, yet always making sure everyone else around me was.

My gaze drops to the shelving next to me. A lot of my mom's stuff is here. A pair of shoes, her raincoat, and what appears to be a sleepover bag. I open it to discover some makeup, a hairbrush, a toothbrush, and toothpaste. *Why would she have a bag here at the beach house? Didn't they just use the stuff they had here or bring it over before staying?*

The door to inside the house opens behind me, pulling me away from my thoughts. I turn to see my mom. She closes the door behind her and takes a seat next to me.

"Boy, it's really uncomfortable here. It's your birthday, sweetheart." She wraps her arm around my waist, pulling me to lean into her. I know I can always count on my mom as someone to lean on, literally. "Want to talk about it?" she asks.

I exhale. "It's Zayn," I say, showing her the napkin.

"Oh," she says with surprise.

"Are you shocked by that?" I ask.

She scratches her head, looking a bit perplexed. "I was worried it was going to be about Liam, that's all," she admits.

"Ah, I see. No, I handled Liam just fine. I can't believe I'm admitting this out loud, but I still love Zayn." The tears start pouring out of me.

"Sweetie, he loves you too. Everyone who's anyone around here knows that. Did something happen between you two?" she asks.

I lean forward, using my hands to wipe at my eyes. "Well, I ran into one of his ex-girlfriends at a coffee shop, and she basically told me to expect him to leave me again. That it's his thing."

"Oh dear. You sure it's not just a jealous ex? Have you spoken with him about it?"

I shake my head and stare down at my shoes. "No, I haven't. I didn't want to, honestly. I was so heated. Ugh, it's fine. I don't want to get hurt again anyway. Better to play it safe."

"Autumn, relationships are tough, but if I've learned

anything these past thirty years, it's that communication is extremely important in a healthy relationship."

My eyes shift from my shoes back to my mom. "Mom, why do you have so much stuff here, including a sleepover bag?"

She hesitates for a moment. "The truth is, sweetie, your father and I were separated for a while before your sister passed."

"What?" I ask. "Why? How? You two have a dream marriage."

She shakes her head and lets out a slight chuckle. "All marriages are tough work. Maybe we have a dream marriage because we know when it's right to take breaks. We're not perfect. Far from it, actually."

"Wow. I'm shocked. I had no idea. Breaks? When?"

"Long ago. One was actually right before I got pregnant with you. Your father and I had a lot of differences when it came to Summer. But, after time apart, we rekindled like always and put in the time and effort to make it work. In fact, dealing with the possibility of losing our first daughter is what caused us to need this last break. But I promise you, we're okay," she says. Her arm reaches out to me for a big hug.

"Thank you for telling me this, Mom. I kind of wish you had sooner," I say when she pulls away.

"I don't. It's your life. I respect if you don't believe in second chances. But I guess it feels right to tell you that I don't just believe in them, I believe they should happen frequently in a marriage." She stands to her feet. "Honey, let's get you inside to your birthday party or else we'll have to ask your friends for a second chance."

AFTER A FEW HOURS of spending time with family and friends along with eating and drinking all my favorite things, the party comes to an end. I say the final goodbye and close the door behind me.

"Whew, that was a lot of fun. Thank you both for throwing me such a fabulous party. Today was a really good day," I say to Natalie and Mason.

They exchange glances with each other. "The celebrations aren't done just yet," Natalie says.

"Oh? What's next?" I ask.

"Whoa, I love how you don't even stress over plans anymore. Adventure suits you," Mason says.

"Thanks," I say. "So, you going to tell me what's next or what?"

"Oh, right, duh. Well, my boyfriend Adam owns a tattoo parlor, so we set up an appointment for the three of us to get tattoos!"

"Really?" I ask.

Mason grabs my hand and holds it in his. "That's right. On your birthday, you get to cross off the very last item on your WOLO list."

"Eeek! Let's go! I'm ready," I say already heading to the door.

"Wait for us!" Natalie says behind me. "Oh, shot gun!" She sticks her tongue out at Mason playfully.

"Hey, you never opened your gift from Zayn. Are you going to?" Mason asks.

"Oh shoot, I totally forgot. Honestly, I'm enjoying the distractions from him. I already cried over him once today. That feels like it's enough."

They both nod. Mason turns up the volume of the radio and we all sing our hearts out to throwback 90s and early 2000s songs. My absolute favorite.

After about a fifteen-minute drive, we arrive at a place called *Adam's Bats and Tats, INKorporated.*

"Hmm, interesting business name. What's up with the 'bats' part?" I ask right before we walk in.

Mason smiles mischievously. "You'll see."

We enter Adam's parlor, and it looks like a weird combo of Hot Topic and a doctor's office. If they were both celebrating Halloween. "Oh, okay. So, your man really likes bats, I take it."

My eyes widen when a man dressed as a bat comes out to the counter to help us. I flash Mason an 'Are you serious?' look, but he doesn't seem to bat an eye! *Ha! Wish I could share that one out loud, but now's clearly not the time.* I look to Natalie for support instead and she seems equally terrified. *Thank God it's not just me.*

"Hi, are you Adam?" I ask breaking the silence.

The bat shakes its head. "Adam will be right with you. In the meantime, I need an ID and for you to fill out this paperwork. Pens are here." He points to a bat-shaped box holding pens that mimic vials of blood.

"Oh okay, cool." I get out my driver's license and turn towards Mason and Natalie. "You guys are getting tattoos, too, right?"

"Actually, no. We sort of told you that preemptively planning on you to say no. You certainly surprised us with agreeing right away," Natalie explains. "But it's on us. Happy birthday!"

I mask my discomfort with a smile. "Thank you, guys. I'm a little sad we aren't all getting them, but—believe it or not—I'm looking forward to it. Once I realized Summer, even from the afterlife, was making me do this, I've had a lot of time to think about what I want."

"That's great," Mason says. "Adam promised to make your first time super special. And we'll be right next to you the whole time for support."

"Thanks," I say.

I finish filling out the paperwork and a guy without a bat costume comes out from the back. He extends a hand to me, "Hey there, you must be Autumn. Nice to meet you. I'm Mason's boyfriend, Adam."

I shake his hand with relief that a bat is not giving me a tattoo tonight. "So great to finally meet the one who's stolen our Mason's heart. Thanks for doing this for me."

"No trouble at all. Let's get you to the back and I'll draw out a description of what you want, you tell me how to tweak it, and then once you're happy and ready, we'll get started." Adam motions for us to follow him to the back. I leave the clipboard of paperwork on the counter for the bat and swipe my ID back before shit gets weirder.

Adam and I agree on one of his drawings and he tells me that he'll be right back.

"Okay, so I know I've changed and was excited to do this, but I won't lie, I'm starting to freak out. What if I hate it or it's too painful? My anxiety is skyrocketing right now," I tell my friends.

Mason offers me some water and Natalie offers me a Xanax. I give her a look because I usually stick to my Lexapro for anxiety, but I've also never gotten a tattoo before. Plus, I have gotten high with Zayn now. And it's my birthday and almost a literal new year so . . . new year, new me, right? I accept it quickly before I change my mind. She hands me her water bottle, and I swallow it down along with the massive lump in my throat.

"So, let me get this straight. You've completed almost

the entire WOLO list, but are chickening out with getting a tattoo?" Natalie asks.

"Did I ask for judgment?" I snap back at her. She flinches. "Sorry, I'm so on edge. And you're right. I've done everything on that list, I'm not going to let a tattoo hold me back from accomplishing all of it now." I take a few deep breaths when Adam returns with a handheld needle gun. I admit to myself that it doesn't look as scary as I had been imagining.

My friends keep me distracted in conversation as Adam needles a design on my left arm. It hurt a bit at first, but honestly, I'm pretty used to the feeling now. I'm having so much fun with Mason and Natalie I sometimes forget I'm even getting a tattoo.

About two hours later, Adam says he's finished. "Alright, my dear. Go ahead and check it out in the mirror. No colors or fill ins, right?"

"Right," I say. "Just the black ink. For now, anyway."

"Yup, you'll soon discover how addicting tattoos can be. You'll be back in here for color and then some," Natalie says. "We should totally all get best friend ones next!"

"Maybe. Let's see how my first one looks first before I make any promises on more." I head over to the mirror to approve of Adam's artwork. I take a look and my breath escapes me for a moment. It's perfect.

It's an orchid and a wildflower interlaced.

Natalie comes over to have a look in the mirror with me. "Oh my God, girl, it's gorgeous! Why'd you choose those flowers?" she asks.

"It started as a joke, but I'm the orchid and Summer is the wildflower. But now, even though she's gone, we're intertwined. I'm no longer just an orchid, I'm a wildflower, too."

23

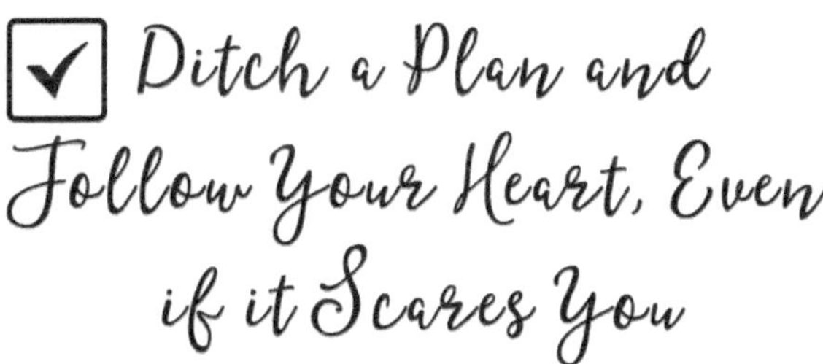

☑ Ditch a Plan and Follow Your Heart, Even if it Scares You

Dear Autumn,

If you're reading this letter now, it means you have completed the list. You did it, Tum Tum! I'm so proud of you, little sis. I hope you feel proud of yourself, too. You've always been brave; you just never knew it yourself. A little secret is that I've always been a tiny bit jealous of how brave you are. I'm sure you're shaking your head in disbelief right now, but it's true. You are brave because even though you preferred routine and predictability, you always handle the unpredictable things life throws at you like a champ. That's right, Autumn Rose Parker, you embrace change. I hoped you'd discover it for yourself though. Speaking of which, I have a strange feeling you THINK you did the last item on the list, *but that you probably haven't. Have you followed your heart or are you playing it safe?*

Knowing you, as I do best, you did this list for me . . . not for you. So, as you saw from the added item on the WOLO list, my last dying wish is for you to take a risk and follow your heart, not a plan. Remember: doing something for yourself that makes you happy is not selfish.

Love you forever and always,
Summer

PS. Are you and Zayn finally together now or what? That man loves you, and we all know you feel the same way. Even if you won't admit it yet.

I sob into my pillow and my mom strokes my hair. "There, there, sweetheart. Let it out," she says.

Coming up for air with tears plastering hair to my face, I wipe at my eyes. "Mom, this is all I have left of her now."

"Oh no, dear. That is so not true. Summer is all around us and inside each of us. I believe she's here with us right now." My mom grabs the box of tissues from my dresser.

"I—I thought—" I say through the sobs, "I really thought that doing the list would somehow bring her back." Mom hands me some tissues, and I pat my eyes dry.

"I had a feeling you might feel that way. Trust me, I've cried every day, and sometimes I wake up thinking she isn't really gone. That she's just been away on one of her trips or adventures for a while," she tells me.

"Yeah," I let out a small laugh. "I actually thought she may have pulled some elaborate scheme and would show up at my birthday party yesterday. It's silly, but I occasionally glanced at the door, hoping to see her come in."

Mom rubs my back and leans in for a hug. "Oh, Autumn. Me too. Your father and I have driven ourselves crazy with the dream she'll come home one day. I'm so sorry. It's so much to carry. But we all know Summer loved us, and I can guarantee she's looking down at us from Heaven, cheering us on in everything we do. Especially everything you do. She may have been a free spirit, but that girl was so protective of you."

A slight smile spreads across my face. "I remember." I take a deep breath and nod. "I love you, Mom. I know I hated the idea of moving back here, but it's been worth it. This is my home."

Mom nods and her lips form a smile, too. "Well, as they always say, home is where the heart is." She stands to her feet and says, "Speaking of hearts, you still need to open Zayn's present."

"Really, Mom?" I scoff.

She picks it up off the floor and brings it to the bed, next to me. "Yes, really. It's your birthday weekend and the boy bought you a present. The least you can do is open it." She chuckles. "Not to mention, I'm curious to see what he got you, too."

"Ahh, I see. So, nosiness is getting the best of you, huh?" I tease.

"Oh hush, silly girl. Just open it."

I pull the bag closer and take out the tissue paper. At the bottom of the bag, there's a black velvet box. The kind that typically holds jewelry. I let out a heavy sigh, holding the box in my hands. I open it and see a charm bracelet. Not just any charm bracelet, but one with a familiar heart charm that I recognize. "Oh my God," I say out loud.

Mom looks at me, eyebrows raised.

"It's the bracelet he gave me for my eighteenth birthday when we were dating." A tear rolls down my cheek. My mind instantly goes back to the night of the breakup when I took it off my wrist and gave it back to him. "He—he kept it. After all this time."

"I don't remember all those extra charms on it though, sweetie. Are you sure?" Mom asks.

I nod, looking at each of the new charms. A silver bull, chopsticks, beach umbrella, a car, a dancer, a taco, roll of toilet paper, and . . . an axolotl? It hits me. I laugh through my tears and tell my mom, "He got me charms to represent all the WOLO adventures we've been on together."

"How sweet!" she says.

I nod, staring at the bracelet.

"Autumn, dear. You need to talk to him. That boy loves you so much." Her words match those in Summer's last letter. *Has everyone known he's been in love with me but me?*

"I can't ask him to do that. It's fine, Mom. I'm fine. Just like Summer, I'm thankful for these memories we do have together. That's what matters."

"Okay, just remember what Summer and that Drake, or whatever, guy always said back when you were in high school. You only live once."

I DECIDE to be brave one last time and to complete the final item on the WOLO list: to follow my heart, even though it scares me.

It starts to rain, so I quickly run up to the front porch to dry off a bit under the overhang. I knock on the door, unsure of what to expect. A moment later, Riley opens it.

"Hi, Ms. Parker. What are you doing here?"

"Um, I just need to speak with your father for a bit. Is he home?" I ask.

Riley peeks her head around me. "No. But he will be soon. Want to come in and wait?"

"Autumn?" I hear Zayn's voice behind me. I turn around to face him, noticing he's soaking wet from the rain too.

Not taking my eyes from Zayn, I turn my head slightly back to Riley. "Never mind, Riley. Thank you."

"No problem," she says. "You guys gonna come inside or—?"

"It's fine, Ri. Shut the door, please. I'll come in soon," Zayn tells her.

She says a quick "okay" before closing the door behind her.

I stare into his eyes through the rain, hesitating to find the words I practiced on my way here. *Maybe I'll just tell him I think I left something here.* My heart beats a million miles a minute inside my chest.

He interrupts my thoughts to ask, "What are you doing here?"

"I uh—I'm here to talk. I realized I messed up with us. Zayn, I told you I trusted you, but then the minute I get a shred of doubt, I run. That's not real trust."

His left eyebrow arches. "Wait. You came here to apologize?"

"Yes," I say.

His eyes squint from the rain before he releases a chuckle. He shakes his head. "Autumn, I'm the one who's sorry. We moved too fast, and I did tell you we would just be friends, and I—well, I showed up at your birthday party thinking that would be my best chance to tell you it's fine, but then I saw Liam there. Figured you guys were getting back together."

"Zayn, stop. None of that is true. Liam and I are never getting back together. He doesn't deserve a fight or a second chance." The sound of the rain grows louder. I speak up, "But you do."

"I do?" he asks.

"Yes. See, the truth is, that day at Eat & Sweets, your ex, Tori, came up to me and told me that you broke things off with her the same way you did with me back in high school. And when I realized you could do that to me again, I got scared."

"Tori? Dear God, I had no idea. I'm so sorry. She and I were a bad match, and I handled it poorly. We never should've dated for as long as we did." He runs his hand through his soaking wet hair. "But this has nothing to do with her. This is about you and me. I messed up when we were younger. I didn't know what the hell I was doing back then," he says.

"And you do now?" I tease. "Do you really only want to be friends?"

He grows serious. "Absolutely not. I want you, Autumn." He inches closer to me. So close that I might just kiss him. "I've never stopped wanting you."

A tear rolls down my cheek after that admission. He grabs my face in his hands and uses his thumbs to wipe away the rain and tears before kissing me. The rain is cold but my whole body is on fire.

I kiss him back harder, finally feeling free. Free from fear. Following my heart.

We pull away and he says, "Let's get under a bit of shelter, shall we?"

We make our way to the front door overhang. He holds my face in his hands again. I reach mine up to grab his. Zayn catches a glimpse of the charm bracelet around my wrist.

"Ah, glad to see you did get my birthday present after all," he says.

I smile and nod. "I did. Thank you. I can't believe you kept it all this time."

"It was the one piece of you I had left to hang onto. I never wanted to let you go. You've always been it for me."

Standing on my tippy toes, I climb up to reach Zayn's ear and whisper, "I love you, Zayn Mitchell. Always have and always will."

He kisses me on the forehead and tells me, "I love you too, Autumn Parker."

THE NEXT DAY Zayn shows up at my door with pizza and a bottle of champagne.

My left eyebrow raises with curiosity. "Oh, are we celebrating something?" I ask.

He chuckles to himself. "Yeah, you finally not hating my guts."

"I never *hated* you, just greatly disliked you." My hand falls to my hip. "I mean, come on, you'd have felt the same if you were practically ghosted by your first love, too." We make our way into the kitchen, and he sets the pizza and bottle down on the counter.

Zayn shrugs. "I mean, I didn't go without suffering either."

I roll my eyes. "Oh yeah?"

"Yeah," he says. His voice grows low when he asks, "Are you happy?"

"Yes, very much so, why?" My eyebrows fold in confusion.

"Like you followed your heart happy?"

I pause for a moment, smirking to myself. "Yeah, I'd say that."

He pulls out the WOLO list from his pocket and grabs the closest pen off the counter and hands it to me. "You should have the honors of your final check."

Grabbing the pen and WOLO list, I exhale and add a final check to Summer's addition.

"How good does that feel, Miss Parker? You got through the entire WOLO list."

I smile. "Definitely couldn't have done it without you," I say before allowing my eyes to fall on his tantalizing lips.

He nods his head and his lips part for a moment, but he doesn't say a word. He tucks a strand of my hair behind my ear before bending down to whisper, "My love for you has never faded, not even once. And when I saw you again here at Meet the Teacher Night, I knew I couldn't stand to let you go again."

I start to melt at his words. He kisses me hard, and I sink into my heels. When he pulls away, I lean into his chest, embracing the man I've been too afraid to admit I love. My hands fall to his, which interlock with mine before he brings one up, kissing the back of it softly.

"Ready to eat?" he asks.

I tug his hand, leading us toward the bedroom. My head turns back as I flash him a flirtatious smile. "You up for one more adventure first?"

Zayn grins from ear to ear. "WOLO."

Epilogue

"**B**abe!" I yell out to Zayn after watching him grab some other girl's butt through my goggles under the water. Swimming next to the girl, he looks at her, then at me, and then back to the girl whose ass he just grabbed.

"Oh shit, my bad. I am so so sorry. I thought you were . . ." He starts to nervously make his way back to me.

When he gets close enough, I wallop the back of his head with my hand. The hand that wears the diamond ring he used to propose to me with last night. We've been here for a few days now, celebrating both my birthday and our one-year anniversary in the Grand Cayman Islands—where we're both swimming with sea turtles and he's apparently grabbing random girls' butts.

"Hey!" he says as he moves his goggles up to the top of his head. He looks at me and smiles, holding up both hands above the water. "Okay, fair enough. I deserve that shit. But you have to know, it really was an accident."

"Mhmm," I say playfully. *Her suit does look almost identical to mine, but I won't admit that to him.*

He moves my goggles to the top of my head so he can see my eyes. "I promise to make it up to you the minute we get back to the hotel room." He winks at me.

"You better," I say. A couple of sea turtles swim past us

so we both put our goggles and snorkels back on to keep swimming with them.

After another hour of swimming with the turtles, followed by dinner at a restaurant in the resort, we finally make our way back into the room—both of us too full to move.

"That sushi was so freaking good," I say, plopping my body down onto the bed.

"Hey, you knocked over the towel animal," Zayn says jumping and landing next to me. He grunts. "Full is an understatement right now. Also, I love how I was the first one to see you try sushi and now it's one of your favorites."

"Yeah, yeah." My hand rests on my stomach and I close my eyes. "This year was the best year of my life."

"That's because we've kept to the WOLO motto." Zayn gets up from the bed and pulls out a piece of paper. "Speaking of WOLO, I'm crossing sea turtles off our list. Only one thing remains."

"Which one?" I ask.

"Sex while turtles watch," he deadpans.

"Wait—what?" I bend my neck to look at his face. I see a smirk go across it. "Ha ha, very funny," I say, tossing a pillow at him.

He grabs the pillow and throws it back on the bed. "Are we gonna pillow fight?"

My eyes widen. "I just might have enough energy to do it, so yes!"

"Wait!" he tells me. "Perfect, because that's the last item on this year's list."

I grab a pillow and jump up on the bed, ready to win this fight with my fiancé.

Dear Summer,

I can't believe it's been one year since my last birthday when I read your final letter. I know you'll never read this, but maybe there is some type of messaging system in Heaven, alerting you that I'm writing this to you now. I miss you every day. Life without you feels strange, but just as Mom and Dad do, I believe you're always with me.

I thought it'd be fun to update you on my life now. A lot has changed. That's right . . . I said change. I still get a little uncomfortable with the idea of change, but I am embracing it more than ever now.

So, first things first. You'd love to hear that I took your advice. I allow myself to follow my heart, even though I'm still terrified to do so. And I've been practicing lots of self-care and not feeling the slightest bit self-ish. See? I listen. Well, sometimes anyway.

A big update is that Zayn and I have been together for a year now, and WE'RE ENGAGED! After months of him begging (kidding), I finally said yes. We are currently vacationing in the Grand Cayman Islands, celebrating our first anniversary.

Oh, and what you'll be most excited to learn is that we now create our own WOLO adventure list every year. It's kept things really exciting. I've done a lot of things I never anticipated, like eating snake, shark fishing, and riding an elephant. We're planning our next list as we speak.

All in all, life is good. I'm still teaching, but instead of holding onto the mindset that I have to stick to it since it's the career I originally chose, I'm okay with the possibility of doing something else in the future. As for now, I'm still at Lake View Elementary, teaching with Mason. He misses you too, by the way.

P.S. Zayn and I plan to get married right on the beach back at home. An intimate wedding with just family and close friends. And as crazy as it sounds, we're doing it in the middle of next summer, in honor of you— my Summer, my wildflower, my friend, and my sister.

That's it for now. As seasons change, so do I. I'll write to you again soon.

See you where the wildflowers grow.
Love forever and always,
Autumn

Author's Note

THANK you for taking the time to read my book.

If you enjoyed it, I'd love for you to leave a review on Amazon, Goodreads, or social media. You can find me on Instagram **@authormandymaree** and Facebook at **Author Mandy Maree**. Sign up for exclusive content, learn about new releases, and get to know more about me and my latest adventures at **authormandymaree.com.**

Acknowledgments

To my wonderful husband, who never blinks twice when it comes to all my (sometimes crazy!) ideas and chasing after my dreams. Thank you for everything. Riding the waves of life has been the best with you. I love you to the moon and back (that's no moon . . .).

To Ania Ray and my writing sisters at Quill & Cup, this book wouldn't exist without you. You've provided me with the space, honor, education, and love to accomplish my writing goals and beyond. All the women there are empowering, and I'm eternally grateful for you all. Specific shoutouts to my original BFFs, Ellie and Lilly. To those I get to see IRL, Tracey and Kase. To those so far, but so close in heart—Bestie, Elze, and Nicole. To the midnight prickles who stayed up late writing, laughing, and putting on facial masks for funsies with me. The Colorado retreat hedgies—Ania, AKA, Tracey, Rachel, Carrie, Kase, and Z. My Arkansas retreat hedgie sisters—Ania, Carrie, Krysann, Mandi, Lauren, Danni—you all watched me transform from my caterpillar-self into a beautiful butterfly, and it meant more than you'll ever know.

To Amanda K, for loving me and my story, talking things out whenever I needed, and being such a fantastic friend.

To the best of friends for asking me about my book and supporting me no matter what—Melissa, Whitney, Lauren, Tara, Annika, Lisa, and Brittany.

To my llama squad besties—Lucy, Tracey, and

Cheyenne—you all have been more supportive than my favorite bra. I enjoy every time we spend together and couldn't ask for a better support system in writing and in life.

To my amazing editor, Alyse Bailey, thank you for taking so much time to help make this book the best it can be. You gave the best feedback, cheered me on when I needed it, and were so flexible when life got crazy.

To the best and most talented illustrator and graphic designer on Earth, Anouk from Another View. You made Zayn and Autumn literally come to life. Your work is beautiful as your soul, and I cannot wait for future designs by you!

To Amanda B (not the OG – haha) for taking the time to format my book, talk through life and stories with me, and laugh our asses off. One day when I see you again, we'll veg out with romance novels, a cup of tea, McDonald's French fries, and reminisce about your suitcase rolling down a hill.

To my teacher friends, who supported me when life and teaching were beyond difficult, and I was reaching the ultimate burnout. Krista, Angelia, and Kevin—my last teaching team—thanks for your support. I couldn't have survived as long as I did without you.

To my ARC team, thank you all for taking the time to read and review *Meet the Teacher*. You guys are simply the best.

To the teachers I've taught with in the past and maybe will teach with in the future, but most importantly, to those who are teaching in the present. Stay strong, my friends. Sending love!

To all the students I've previously taught. You are brilliant, bold, beautiful, and kind and don't let anyone convince you otherwise. Even if you grow up and feel that you never made an impact on anyone else's life, please know you have on mine.

A huge thank you to all my family, especially my mom and dad for being supportive in anything I choose to pursue. My in-laws, aunts, and uncles who always shine bright in a dark world. And to my guardian angel grandparents, I miss you all very much and wish you could be here to celebrate with me.

A final thank you to my kids. To my angel baby, A—I love you even though I never met you. And to my own little wildflowers—M & W—I love you, and I can't wait to watch you grow up and accomplish all your own dreams and more!